Little Durango

*Being the Personal Memoir of
Gabriela Falcón and a True Account of the
Taming of the Arizona Borderlands
(1869 - 1900)*

Historical Fiction by
MW Ashe

ARCHER TRENT, PUBLISHER

Illuminated Large-Print Edition
ISBN 978-1-7347814-2-7

COVER PHOTOGRAPH
"Arizona Female Scout '86" (detail)
A Frank Randall Photographs of Apache Indians 1888
THE HUNTINGTON DIGITAL LIBRARY
Image Number: photCL 101 (79)
Unique Digital Identifier: 415473

This novel, a literary project of the Griffoun Society of Houston, Texas, is as accurate a history as can be told through a work of fiction. No liberties have been taken with established facts.

To Lucasta, Going to the Wars

Richard Lovelace

Tell me not (Sweet) I am unkind,
    That from the nunnery
Of thy chaste breast and quiet mind
    To war and arms I fly.

True, a new mistress now I chase,
    The first foe in the field;
And with a stronger faith embrace
    A sword, a horse, a shield.

Yet this inconstancy is such
    As you too shall adore;
I could not love thee (Dear) so much,
    Lov'd I not Honour more.

CHAPTER I
FORT BOWIE, ARIZONA TERRITORY
1886

Arizona Female Scout was the label that Mr A Frank Randall scrawled on the cabinet-card portrait he made of me at Fort Bowie. Of course, that title was a bit of a misnomer, for I was not, in fact, an army scout. Indeed, I had, that very day, been turned down for the scouting job I had hoped to secure. The stuffy old colonel that interviewed me insisted that it was not because of my sex but simply because General Crook already had a full complement of Apache scouts (fifty in number), not to mention a chief scout (Mr Al Sieber) and several assistant chiefs, all of whom were Anglo-American men. What the colonel did not put into words but seemed to imply was the question: *What possible use would the army have of a seventeen-year-old Mexican girl, even if her dubious claim to being able to ride, shoot, and track like an Apache were actually true?*

"Why don't you come to work for me instead?" Mr Randall suggested. "I've been hanging about this fort for days trying to get someone to guide me to some of the more remote Indian camps."

"You want to take pictures of the Apaches where they live. Is that it?" I asked.

"I already have a pretty sizable collection of indigene portraits, but most were made in a studio or at one fort or another. I think the images to be captured at a village far removed from White society might be of an entirely different quality."

"If I agree to work for you, will you teach me photography? I could be a big help to you if I knew what to do."

"You're interested in taking pictures yourself, are you?"

I nodded vigorously. I had long been intrigued with the art of photography and its related sciences. "I once had my portrait made in Tombstone. I've been fascinated with photography ever since."

"So you know Mr CS Fly?"

"I do know him, but it was Mrs Fly that took my picture."

"I didn't realize that Mrs Fly was a photographer too, but I suppose it makes sense. Someone has to run their portrait business whilst he's gallivanting all over the country. I believe that he stays in the field sometimes for weeks at a stretch."

"I've seen some of the landscape pictures he's made and portraits of soldiers and captured Apaches. I like those images a lot."

Not to be eclipsed by CS Fly, Mr Randall mentioned that he too had accompanied General Crook in pursuit of Geronimo. "But in truth, I usually manage to get better pictures when I am entirely on my own."

"Except for the fact that you need a guide," I reminded him. "Hire me to be your assistant photographer, and I'll take you anywhere you want to go. No one knows this country better than I do."

The offer he made me was so modest that, were I any less eager to learn photography, I should have been insulted. To sweeten the deal, however, he allowed me to keep the fringed leather jacket he had furnished for me to pose in. It had been left in his wagon accidentally by a young woman whose portrait he had made in New Mexico Territory, and he knew not how to return it to her. It was beautifully decorated with Navajo ribbon work. I accepted happily, and we shook hands to seal our arrangement.

On the trail, over the next few days, my new boss and mentor coaxed from my lips the story of my life. In particular, he wanted to know how I had come to be at Fort Bowie seeking employment as an army scout.

CHAPTER II
RANCH LIFE
1869 - 1875

I was born in 1869 on a little ranch near Santa Fe, New Mexico Territory. My full legal name is *Hilda Gabriela Jesusita Falcón*. Throughout my early childhood, I was called *Gaby*, which nickname I eventually came to hate, the reason being that *Gaby* sounds exactly like *gabby*, suggesting that I talk too much. I can promise you, I do not. Following the example of my father, who is the most dignified man I have ever known, I speak only when I have something important to say. I despise foolish prattle.

At the age of eleven, I acquired another nickname: *Little Durango*. Although bestowed upon me by a man I hated, this particular cognomen I do quite like. If it is all the same to you, *Little Durango* is how I should like to be thought of from now on. My father, you see, is called *Durango*, for long ago—before I was born—he was employed as a *vaquero* and *pistolero* in the Mexican state of Durango.

Later, drifting northward, he met and fell in love with my mother Consuela Neri, a granddaughter of Ignacio Perez, once a rich and powerful *ranchero*. Unfortunately, my Perez forebears had, in 1830, been driven from their land by marauding Apaches, but the Perez descendants, including my mother, still retained ownership of more than seventy-three thousand acres on both sides of the Mexican border. When my mother died in childbirth barely a year after eloping with my father, her portion of ownership of the storied Rancho San Bernardino fell to me; although, in my childhood, of course, I knew nothing of the magnificent inheritance I was due.

In any event, at the time of my birth, there happened to be in Santa Fe a thirteen-year-old

Apache girl called *Madre de Dios* (*Mother of God*) with a new baby of her own. I was given to her to nurse, and she became my surrogate mother. Madre de Dios was the wife of Cicero the blacksmith, a former slave. Their son Horace became a brother to me.

My father, devastated by the loss of his young wife, now lavished all his attention on me. He adored me, and I, in return, absolutely worshiped him. The first few years of my life were, therefore, idyllic. I was pampered and spoiled as no child, save a royal princess, had ever been.

When Cicero died of small pox, Papa took the blacksmith's widow to be his new wife, adopting three-year-old Horace to be his son. I do not believe that Madre de Dios and my father were ever in love. Their union was an arrangement of convenience. She needed a husband, her son needed a father, Papa needed a wife, and I needed continuity. This solution answered all those needs.

Papa, in those days, worked variously as a lawman, a brand inspector, an army scout, or a shotgun messenger. Many of his assignments kept him on the trail for weeks at a time. I grew up thinking of him as a knight errant. I still have the badge he fashioned for himself from a silver *cinco-peso* coin. He was a close friend to former Texas Ranger John Horton Slaughter and cattleman John Chisum. In fact, Papa, Mr Slaughter, and Mr Chisum often played poker together. Also within their circle of friendship were ranchers Charles Goodnight and Oliver Loving and brothers Lewis Warren Neatherlin and James Franklin Neatherlin (cousins of Mr Slaughter).

In 1873, we relocated to Arizona Territory. Entrepreneur Henry Clay Hooker, having recently established Sierra Bonita Ranch in the Sulphur Springs Valley, hired Papa as a range detective to help protect his vast herds from rustlers. My earliest clear memory is of the journey we made from the place of my birth to our new home. We were on the trail for days. Madre de Dios drove a heavily laden wagon as Papa rode ahead scouting the trail. Some days, he set me in front of him in the saddle; other times, he took Horace, and I had to be content to bump along with Madre de Dios.

Along the way, each of the two adults pointed out to Horace and to me landmarks by which to orient ourselves in the future, recounted stories of days gone by, and instructed us on reading sign. Madre de Dios was especially gratified by how eager I was to learn all that she had to teach me of Indian lore and wilderness skills. Her own son Horace was never half as attentive as I was.

"You're a good little Apache," she told me with a laugh when, by examining horse droppings one day, I was able to estimate accurately how recently an unknown rider had crossed our trail.

But please do not imagine that Madre de Dios was in any way disappointed in Horace, who listened obediently and made something of an effort to absorb instruction and yet could never manage to muster any real enthusiasm. She accepted Horace for who he was and loved him unconditionally, and he knew it. In later years, Horace would be the better-read of us, the more intellectual, as I should, of course, be the more adept at horsemanship, marksmanship, tracking, and wilderness survival.

Sierra Bonita Ranch was enormous. Dime novels often portray cattle ranches as consisting of a little ranch house, a bunk house for bachelor herdsmen, a barn, and a few stock enclosures. I suppose that may be true for family-run subsistence ranches, but Mr Hooker's ranch was a major operation, requiring the support of a vast community of workers with various skills: cooks, butchers, seamstresses, laundresses, saddlers and cobblers, farmers and gardeners, carpenters, farriers, gunsmiths, horse wranglers, and others, each family abiding in its own little *jacal.*

Hundreds of acres were devoted to producing hay for the winter. There were food crops too, as well as hogs, chickens, and goats for consumption on the ranch itself. A big-business ranch community is very like a small town. The human population of Sierra Bonita Ranch far exceeded a hundred. There was even a school for the children. That's where Horace and I learned to read and write and do sums.

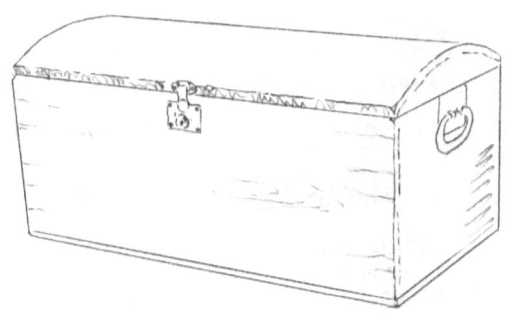

CHAPTER III
RUSTLERS AND HOODOOS
1875 - 1876

I shall never forget the day the letter came. I watched Papa read it, and I saw his face turn deadly serious. I felt sure that my life was about to change and not for the better. Refolding the letter and returning it to its envelope, Papa rose slowly to his feet, strode grim-faced to his gun chest, unlocked it, and began selecting firearms therefrom.

On the floor beside the chest, he laid a Sharp's long-range rifle and a saddle scabbard for it, two Army Colts in a double-shoulder-holster rig, several bandoleers, boxes of ammunition, and a Smith and Wesson Model 3 break-top revolver (the mate to the one he always wore on his right hip).

In a saddle scabbard on his horse, Papa already had a Henry repeating rifle. One rifle and one pistol were all he usually carried. Why on earth did he suddenly feel the need for so many guns? It looked to me as if he were arming himself for war. After carefully re-locking the chest with a key that he normally kept in his own pocket, he offered that key to Madre de Dios, who was clearly as alarmed as I was.

"¿Qué pasó, mi esposo?" she asked. "What has happened? And what do you do now?"

To Horace and me, she usually spoke in the Apache tongue, but with Papa, who understood not a word of her native language, she employed a curious mix of Spanish and English, neither of which she commanded very well.

"A good friend, a friend of many years," Papa replied, "is in trouble and needs my help. I have to go to Texas for a while. I'll ask Mr Hooker if you can remain here whilst I am away. Otherwise, go to Los Neri two days to the south in Sonora. The Neris are Gaby's relatives. They will welcome you, I think. They have never met

Gaby, but I expect that they will be keen to get to know her."

"No," Madre de Dios said firmly. "I go to my own people. You return, you find us at village of Cochise."

Cochise himself had died of cancer the previous year, a scant two years after signing the peace treaty that ended his eleven-year war with the Whites. But if Papa came looking for us on the San Carlos Reservation, then asking directions to the "village of Cochise" would be an effective means of finding us, for while there are many Apache camps, there is but one directly identified with Cochise, the great chief known to his people as the *Man of Oak.*

"The children need to be in school," Papa reminded Madre de Dios gently, then added diplomatically, "but of course, you must do as you think best."

Papa knew that Madre de Dios, who was herself completely illiterate, fully appreciated the value of education. She was ever so proud of Horace and me for having learned how to read and write. Mind you, at six years of age, we were not

yet very accomplished. In any event, Madre de
Dios accepted that it would be a disservice to allow
our schooling to be interrupted.

"*Bien,*" she agreed. "They stay in school."

Papa held her face between his hands and
kissed her on the mouth, then knelt to hug Horace
to his chest.

"Be a good boy, Horace. Take care of your
mother and your sister. I'm counting on you."

Freeing himself from Papa's embrace, Horace
offered Papa his hand to shake. "I'll do my best,
sir."

Then it was my turn. Tearfully, I threw my
arms around my father's neck and begged him not
to go. I had not meant to disgrace myself in that
way, but my distress was simply so great that I lost
my head.

"I have to go, Gaby. What kind of a father
would I be if I could not be counted upon to
answer duty's call? What kind of man would I be
if I ignored a plea for help from a valued friend?"

Then lifting me in his arms, he carried me,
still weeping, to the shelf where he kept his dearest
possession, a leather-bound volume of English verse.

He opened the book to a place marked by a pressed flower and read aloud to me a poem by Richard Lovelace.

The sentences being of rather odd construction, I didn't entirely understand the beginning of the poem, but the final two lines made perfect sense, and I was reminded why I so admired my father.

"'I could not love thee, dear, so much, loved I not Honor more.'" I repeated aloud. "I understand, Papa. I really do. I just feel sad that you are going away."

"I know. I'm sad too, Gaby. I want you to keep this book for me. Treat it as your own whilst I am away. And when you return it to me someday, I'll expect you to tell me what other wisdom you have gained from reading it. It is a treasure trove of insights and good thoughts."

"I promise."

Packing up his gear, Papa rode off in the direction of the main ranch house, presumably to offer an abject apology to Mr Hooker for leaving without notice. Then he was on his way to Mason County, Texas, where a range war was brewing.

I suppose that, before I continue the narrative of my childhood, I ought to tell you what I now know about the Mason County War, often referred to as the *Hoodoo War*. Mason County on the northwestern fringe of the Texas Hill Country had been settled by German immigrants, many of whom had established themselves as cattle ranchers. In the mid-1870s, all the biggest ranches in the region were still owned by descendants of the original German settlers, but any number of small ranches were now being run by Anglo-Americans. Papa's friend—I don't believe I ever heard his name—was one of the latter.

Coexistence between the big ranches owned by German-Americans and the smaller ranches owned by Anglo-Americans might never have been a problem had not so many of the small ranches been nothing but fronts for cattle-rustling operations. Honest ranchers were being bled dry. Papa's friend had initially needed Papa's help only in dealing with these rustlers, but by the time Papa arrived in Texas, the situation had become infinitely more complicated with the formation of a Hoodoo Army of night riders, hooded vigilantes, who lynched anyone even vaguely suspected of rustling. Honest small-time ranchers were caught in the middle of what quickly devolved into a race war, as the only evidence of criminality required by the Hoodoos seemed to be non-German ancestry.

Hostilities continued for more than a year and spilled over into Gillespie, Lampasas, and Burnet Counties as well. Officially, casualties (including shootings and lynchings) numbered only twelve, but Papa later told me that he had first-hand knowledge of at least twenty killings. He suspected that the actual number was far greater than that.

Sheriff John Clark, himself a German-American, openly sided with and supported the Hoodoos. When, eventually, the Texas Rangers intervened in force, Clark was arrested.

Incidentally, the most feared gang of rustlers was led by rancher Scott Cooley, himself a former Texas Ranger. The notorious gunman Johnny Ringo was a member of the Cooley Gang, and Papa knew of at least two murders committed by him in Mason County. In December of 1875, Ringo and Cooley were both arrested in Lampasas County. The Cooley Gang promptly raided the jail and freed them. Ringo then left Texas and made his way to Arizona Territory. The following summer, Cooley died of poisoning shortly after dining at the Nimitz Hotel in Fredericksburg. Fredericksburg is in Gillespie County. The Nimitz Hotel is, of course, a German-owned business.

When Peace again took up residence in Mason County, Papa made his way back to Arizona, only to discover that his family was no longer abiding at Sierra Bonita Ranch. Assuming that we must have gone to Los Neri, as he had suggested, Papa turned his horse toward Mexico.

I have no doubt that my father was anxious about having to face the Neris again. They had been resentful of his taking my mother Consuela from them at such a tender age. She had been only fifteen years old when she had run off with Papa, and then, of course, she had died less than a year later. Papa had sent us to the Neris because they were my only blood relatives, besides himself, and because it would be a safe place for us whilst he was in Texas. He felt that he could count on the Neris to extend their hospitality to Madre de Dios and

Horace as well. He doubted that the same welcome would ever again be offered to him.

Indeed, getting me back from the Neris promised to be a monumental challenge. That this powerful family could count on the support of an army of *pistoleros* was not lost on my father. Two of my Neri uncles, you see, were officers in the *rurales*. Even so, Papa was a man of courage; he would have ridden straight through the Gates of Hell in order to be reunited with his family. Of that I am absolutely certain.

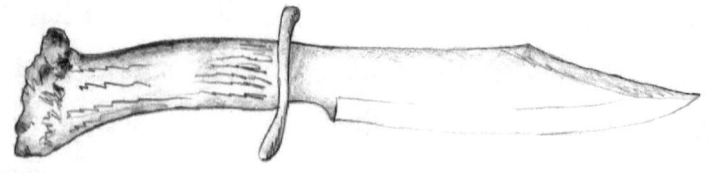

CHAPTER IV
SAN CARLOS RESERVATION
1875 - 1876

Shortly after Papa's departure from Sierra Bonita Ranch, Mr Hooker himself paid a visit to our little *jacal*. He offered Madre de Dios employment cooking and washing for the bachelor stockmen in the bunk house. He did not explicitly state that her acceptance was a condition of our continuing to abide on the ranch, but she understood well enough. We could remain in our quarters, and Madre de Dios would begin receiving wages, or we could be on our way.

"*Sí. Lo hago,*" she agreed. "I do it."

During the day, whilst Horace and I were in school, Madre de Dios did the washing. Then in the afternoon, she would prepare a casserole dinner in a huge cast-iron pot: *cabrito guisado, chili con carne,* beef stew, sausages and beans, *arroz con pollo,* something of that nature. To go with it, she would make a huge stack of tortillas. Then, she and Horace and I together would carry the steaming food and the carefully folded laundry to the bunk house.

The stockmen, by the way, always prepared their own breakfasts, which usually consisted of coffee, bacon, and tortillas left over from the previous day. Eggs were available to them, but only rarely did they avail themselves of that luxury. Somehow, frying bacon was deemed manly, but frying eggs was too domestic a chore. For lunch out on the range or at whatever job they had been assigned, they chewed on jerky or opened some canned fruit from their saddle bags. Madre de Dios was responsible only for their evening meal.

Occasionally, she earned a little extra by darning socks or sewing patches on torn clothing. For this service, the stockmen themselves paid her a few cents or even a nickel. Once, one of them made the mistake of offering her a whole dollar to climb into his bunk with him.

"This woman not whore!" she screamed in his face. I have never seen her so angry. "I wife of Durango. He kill you."

The stockman laughed. "He left you here on your own. You really think he gives a shit about you?"

This insult was too much for Madre de Dios. Drawing her knife, she rushed the man. Happily, someone put out a foot and tripped her before she could commit murder. Most of the dozen or so witnesses were doubled over with laughter.

The man that had intervened knelt, and holding her down, whispered in her ear, "The fool deserves to die. I'll give you that. But if you kill him here and now, his pals there will kill you. They all have guns, and you do not. Hell, if they don't shoot you, they'll hang you. Do you really want to make orphans of your children?"

Madre de Dios took several deep breaths and slowly regained her composure. "I go. *Suélteme.*"

Horace and I had both witnessed the confrontation. Following Madre de Dios back to our *jacal*, we were struggling not to cry, so frightened were we still. And what a foul mood was upon Madre de Dios! I had never seen her like this. She did not speak a word but hitched the horses to the wagon, then began loading our possessions. Silently, Horace and I assisted her. She did not deign to tell us what to do, but we required no instructions. What had to be done was clear enough.

Papa's gun chest was too heavy for the three of us together to lift, so we removed its contents onto the floor. Then Madre de Dios, grunting at the effort, carried it empty to the wagon. Finally, one at a time, we returned all the guns and ammunition to the chest.

It was well after dark when we left the ranch community. Madre de Dios wanted to get us as far away as possible as quickly as possible. We did not stop for the night. Happily, the moon was bright, and the trail was easy to follow, at least for the first twenty miles or so. Apparently, we were heading deep into Apachería. By morning, the trail had dwindled away to almost nothing.

"*Ojala que* wagon wheel no break!" Madre de Dios muttered to no one in particular. By almost any standard, it was a terrible sentence, but I understood what she meant.

Our progress became slower and slower as the way became rockier and more dangerous. Eventually, however, we arrived at our destination and received as warm a welcome as we could have hoped for. Madre de Dios was remembered fondly by many in that camp. Horace and I were curiosities to be gawked at.

"This one is the son of a buffalo soldier?" a girl of about fifteen years asked Madre de Dios of Horace.

"No. His father was a blacksmith."

The girl wrinkled her brow, indicating that she did not understand the meaning of the word *blacksmith*.

"A blacksmith is the one that puts the iron shoes on horses," Madre de Dios explained.

"Ah!" the girl said, enlightened. "*Blacksmith*: it is a difficult word to say, is it not?"

As it turned out, this girl already knew many English words. With me, she made a point to converse daily in English. We had long conversations, just she and I on our own. In almost no time, she was completely fluent in English.

"I am called *Dahteste*," she told me.

"Pleased to meet you," I said offering her my hand to shake. "My name is *Gabriela*. My brother is Horace."

Dahteste appeared not to be familiar with the practice of shaking hands, or perhaps she just thought it inappropriate for girls. Even so, after only a moment's hesitation, she took my hand, and the smile that lit up her face told me that we were now friends. Mind you, she was nine years my senior; I suppose she was more like an aunt to me than a girlfriend, but that was not how it felt to me at the time.

As a twelve-year-old, Dahteste had chosen the warrior's path and had ridden into battle with Cochise. Of course, the war had ended later that same year.

"Do you think Papa will be able to find us here?" I asked Madre de Dios one day. The longer we remained in this remote location, the more concerned was I that I might never see my father again.

"Soon we go to Los Neri," she assured me.

Whilst we remained on the San Carlos Reservation, Dahteste's older sister Ilthgozay was wed to Kalesh, head man of a nearby village. Kalesh, I believe, is known to the Whites as *Chihuahua*. Dahteste herself was, at that time, being courted by a young man named *Ahnandia*.

"I like him sometimes," she confided to me, "but other times, he makes me so angry, I want to kill him."

When, eventually, we prepared to take our leave, Madre de Dios asked around if anyone could give her directions for finding Los Neri.

"I know that place," said Dahteste. "It is near to where *rurales* are stationed. I'll travel with you and guide you."

The journey south was relatively easy, and we made good time. Most nights, we slept out in the open. It is very pleasant to drift off into slumber with stars twinkling overhead. One night, however, it began to rain just at dusk, so we bedded down beneath the wagon.   That too was an agreeable experience, because we all had to snuggle close in order to stay warm and dry.

Unfortunately, our good luck ran out before we reached Los Neri.   In Guadalupe Canyon, where we crossed into Mexico, we ran into trouble. One of our horses went lame, and whilst Madre de Dios and Dahteste struggled to get it out of harness, road agents took us by surprise.   There were two of them.   I didn't know their names, but I recognized them as former stockmen for Henry Hooker.   One, in fact, was the man that had so angered Madre de Dios by offering her money to let him bed her.

"Well, look who we have here," he said, grinning wickedly, when he recognized Madre de Dios.   "You should've took my dollar when I offered it to you.   Now, I'm simply gonna have you fer free.   Then I'm gonna teach you a lesson you'll never forget."

Neither Madre de Dios nor Dahteste had yet been relieved of their sidearms.   Both were wearing long skirts with gun belts around their waists.   I could read in their faces that they were calculating the odds of drawing against men that already had guns out and pointed at them. A third man now appeared. Coming up behind Dahteste, he lifted her revolver from its holster. He then took her knife as well.

The man covering Madre de Dios said, "Now, you drop yours. You and me, we got unfinished business to take care of."

Madre de Dios unbuckled her gun belt and let it fall to the ground.

The man kicked it away. "Now the knife. Where is it?"

Madre de Dios started to put her hand behind her back, but she was halted when the man cocked his revolver and pressed the barrel to her nose.

"Just turn around slowly," he said.

She complied, and he took the sheath knife from the waist band of her skirt and tossed it away.

"Now, turn back around," said the man, holstering his gun.

She did so and was met by a vicious slap across the face. Her shirt was then ripped open to expose her breasts.

Stepping closer, the man put his left hand behind Madre de Dios's neck and pulled her face to his for a kiss. With his right hand, he lifted her skirt and groped between her legs.

"Ow!" he screamed as she bit his lip, drawing blood.

As both his hands went up to his face, Madre de Dios seized the opportunity to snatch the revolver from his holster. Shooting him in the lower belly, she turned the gun toward the other two men, both of whom responded instantly by firing at her. One bullet took her in the forehead; the other, in the center of the chest. There was no doubt whatsoever that she was dead.

Horace fainted. He and I had been standing together by the wagon, watching helplessly. I ran to Madre de Dios, cradled her head in my arms, and wept bitterly. But even in my grief, my teary eyes were searching the ground for the weapon Madre de Dios had dropped. *Where could it be? Beneath her body? Yes, probably.* If I could just get my hands on it, I'd finish what she had started, or I'd die trying.

The man standing before Dahteste turned and walked my way, but his interest was directed at his wounded *compañero*. He gave me hardly a glance. It was inconceivable that a little girl of barely seven years might constitute a serious threat.

Standing over his friend, the man said, "Looks like she's done for you, partner."

"Is the bitch dead?" the wounded man asked though clinched teeth.

"She is."

Although in much pain, the wounded man managed a sardonic smile. "Good!"

"Want me to finish you?"

The man on the ground just nodded, then closed his eyes to await the *coup de grâce*, which was delivered promptly.

Now, the two surviving bandits turned their attention to raping Dahteste. She fought like a wildcat, scratching and biting, but they easily overpowered her. They were not about to make the kind of mistake that their pal had made with Madre de Dios. Whilst one held their victim down, the other hung his gun belt on a nearby tree limb. They then switched rôles. With their firearms safely out of reach, they stripped Dahteste bare. Whilst one pinned her arms above her head, the other dropped his trousers and forced his way between her legs as she lay on her back on the ground. She kicked and bucked, but to no avail.

So engrossed were these men in their evil undertaking that they did not even notice my stealthy approach. Feeling about beneath Madre de Dios's skirt, I had found the revolver with which she had shot her attacker. Holding it behind my back, I got to my feet and crept slowly toward the men scuffling with Dahteste. The gun was far too heavy for me to aim accurately. I knew that I had to get quite close. I was practically on top of them before I fired. Steadying the barrel with my left hand, I shot the man that was raping Dahteste.

The other man scrambled to his feet and was momentarily indecisive whether to rush me or go for his own gun. Dahteste struggled to her hands and knees and managed to put herself between the man and me. Rather than try to get past Dahteste, he dashed to the tree where his gun belt still hung.

I, meanwhile, was trying to reassert my grip on the revolver and cock it again. The report had deafened me and the recoil had jarred me. Before I could raise the barrel once more and point it at my remaining adversary, he had his own gun out and would certainly have shot me dead had not Horace, now recovered from his fainting spell, thrown a rock at the man, distracting him for the split second needed for me to aim and fire again.

Getting to her feet, Dahteste closed the distance between herself and me and took the heavy revolver from my hands. Then still quite naked, she checked to see whether either of the men I had shot was still alive. Both were gravely wounded but breathing yet. Before donning her clothes, Dahteste gathered all the weapons and laid them on the wagon seat.

Stripping the two men of all their clothes, we staked them out spread eagle on the ground and cut their penises off. Tearfully, they begged for mercy, but our hearts were hard toward them. They screamed in agony when we made the cuts. First, Dahteste emasculated the man that had raped her; then she offered me the knife, and I did the same to the other. These men would die slowly, and before they expired, scavengers, such as ravens, coyotes, and buzzards, might well show up to feed on their living flesh, thus making their departure from this world even more horrific.

Dahteste dipped her fingers in the wounds of the men I had shot and marked my forehead and my cheeks with their blood. "You did well, Little Mankiller. Your heart is true Diné."

Diné is how the Apaches refer to themselves as a people. Madre de Dios had once called me *a good little Apache*. Now Dahteste had just said that I had the heart of an Apache. Even in my unspeakable grief, I took pride in being found worthy to be identified with that warrior race.

As Dahteste buried Madre de Dios a mile or so down the trail, Horace and I held each other and wept uncontrollably. The body of the man whom Madre de Dios had shot we left where he had fallen. The following day, we encountered my father on the trail.

Having already been to Los Neri and having been told that we had not been there, he had turned his horse toward the San Carlos Reservation.

I related to him all that had transpired. He was quite distressed to hear about Madre de Dios. He thanked Dahteste for taking care of Horace and me.   Then after concealing the wagon well off the trail, Papa gave Dahteste the remaining horse from the team.   She had been prepared to walk back to the reservation, but Papa would not hear of it.   She bid us farewell and rode off northward.

Then, with me in front of Papa and Horace behind, we rode west and soon came to the little community of Los Neri.   Papa and an uncle of mine, Francisco Neri, then lead a team of mules out to pull the wagon in.

CHAPTER V
Los Neri and Charleston
1876 - 1879

Los Neri, sometimes referred to as *Ranchito Neri,* is not an actual town. There is no store or trading post. There is no post office. There is not even a sign to identify the place to travelers. Nor is Los Neri anything like the Sierra Bonita Ranch community. Almost all the residents here are related to one another, either by blood or through marriage. Even those few individuals employed as household servants or as *vaqueros* are distant cousins. My father, who had been employed here in the late 1860s, was a great great nephew of his *patrón,* my grandfather.

My uncles, Francisco Neri and Felipe Neri, were both officers in the *rurales* (officially *la Guardia Rural*), a mounted police force established in 1861 by Benito Juárez, later to be expanded by Porfirio Díaz. The *rurales* were charged with keeping the peace in the region and enforcing the law. Felipe was *comandante* of an outpost. At seven years of age, I thought my uncles very dashing in their traditional Mexican attire and enormous *sombreros*.

Long ago, Felipe, Francisco, and my father had been *compañeros de bendición*, but upon my father's elopement with my mother, that relationship had been somewhat fractured. Apparently, all was now forgiven. My father was again welcomed into the bosom of the Neri family. Papa, Horace, and I were even given rooms in my grandfather's house, the oldest and largest in the community.

My grandmother had died a few years before, my mother having been her only child. Francisco and Felipe had been born to my grandfather's first wife, who had also died.

After my grandmother's passing, my grandfather had not married again, but he now kept a half-Apache mistress, who had previously been his housekeeper. Her name was *Anavid*. She became our staunch ally and supporter the moment she discovered that my brother and I could converse fluently with her in the Apache tongue.

Horace and I attended classes in a single-room adobe-brick schoolhouse serviced by an itinerant teacher, who was responsible for three small communities in northern Sonora. A month of intense instruction (six long days a week) was followed by two months of idleness. Classes, of course, were conducted in Spanish, which language Horace and I understood well enough, but we had to learn all over again how to spell and how to read, for the orthography and phonetics are quite different than in English. We got along with the other children but did not immediately form any close friendships. Horace and I remained each other's best pal and most trusted confidant.

Horace always said he considered me more of a brother to him than a sister. "Girls are perverse, Gaby, but you're like a boy." I believe that Horace meant to be paying me a compliment, but even at age seven, I did not much care for being told that I was in any way lacking in femininity.

The following year (1877), Papa traveled to Tucson to meet up with his old friend Texas John Slaughter, who was visiting the territory with his wife Eliza and their children. School being out, I begged to be allowed to go along. Papa readily agreed and asked Horace if he would like to come too.

Horace declined the invitation. Recalling our bloody confrontation with highwaymen the year before, he had no desire ever again to go on the trail. And indeed, he has spent his entire life until now within the little community of Los Neri. These days, he teaches school there on a full-time basis. That is to say, he does not ride a circuit, as did our teacher in days of old.

In any event, Papa and I made an uneventful journey, but arrived in Tucson on the very day of Eliza Slaughter's funeral. She had been stricken ill the previous week and had died the day before. Papa hurriedly bought me a dark blue dress for the occasion. He himself always dresses in black, so he needed no special funeral attire, but he bought a new black suit anyway, in order to show utmost respect. This was the first time I ever saw my father wear a tie.

A day after the funeral, Mr Slaughter, Papa, and I, riding three abreast, traveled southeast into an untamed wilderness, which until a few short years before had been the heart of Apache country. We were followed by a wagon in which Mr Slaughter's small children rode. Bringing up the rear was the rest of the Slaughter entourage, consisting of six gunmen. Ordinarily, Mr Slaughter traveled alone, but because he had brought his family on this trip, he had wanted them to have a strong bodyguard. Unfortunately, that bodyguard had been helpless to defend Eliza against small pox.

Mr Slaughter led us to the site of a proposed new cattle ranch. It might take a year or two to sell off his assets in Texas and New Mexico and shut down all operations there. In the meantime, Mr Slaughter needed a trustworthy agent in Arizona Territory to represent his interest here. Papa was to be that man; he was charged with acquiring land along the San Pedro River and arranging for the construction thereon of dwellings, outbuildings, and stock enclosures. Until the project was a little further along, I should have to return to Los Neri. When Mr Slaughter came next to Arizona Territory, he would be driving a great herd of cattle.

In the meantime, other ranchers, including Newman Haynes Clanton and his large family, were setting up operations in the same region. In September of that year, a rich silver strike was made at nearby Goose Flats, and the Tombstone Mining Company was established. Other mining companies were soon formed as well. Around the mines, sprung up a sizable community, which, in 1879, would be named as *Tombstone*.

Ten miles to the southwest was the nearest source of abundant flowing water: the San Pedro River. Here were built the mills to process the ore. Thus, the towns of Millville and Contention City came into being. Directly across the river from Millville would be Charleston, a bedroom community for the mill workers. The Clanton Ranch headquarters, a spacious adobe *hacienda*, was a scant five miles outside Charleston.

As city lots in Charleston became available for purchase, Ike and Phineas Clanton, two of Newman

Clanton's sons, began buying up as much of the town's real estate as they could afford. It was from Ike Clanton that Papa rented rooms in Charleston.

In 1878, Elliot Larkin Ferguson, wanted for robbery in Goliad, Texas, changed his name to *Pete Spence* and set himself up in the cattle business in the general vicinity of Charleston.

Brothers Tom McLaury and Frank McLaury, stockmen employed on the Clanton Ranch, began, in 1879, ranching on their own. They owned no land, but leased from Mr Frank Patterson of Tombstone a small spread near Soldier's Hole far to east of the San Pedro River Valley.

When Mr Slaughter, at last, completed his business in Texas and New Mexico and was preparing to drive his cattle west to his new ranch in Arizona Territory, one of the drovers he hired was Billy Claiborne. Paid off at the conclusion of the drive, Billy found employment with the Neptune Mining Company. For a while he drove a slag cart. Then he learned to operate an amalgamator. But Billy soon fell in with bad company and was drawn into a life of crime.

Arriving with another cattle drive about this time were the already-notorious outlaws Pony Diehl and Curly Bill Brocius, as well as former lawmen Sherman McMaster and Turkey Creek Jack Johnson. Curiously, these four men, who had previously been on opposite sides of the law, seemed now to be on very friendly terms with one another. Sherman McMaster, in fact, had once arrested Brocius. Apparently, Brocius held no grudge for that affront.

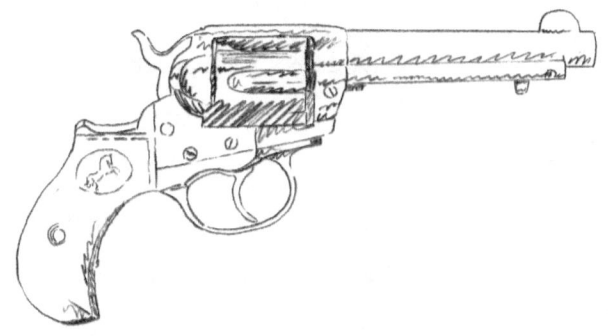

CHAPTER VI
COWBOYS AND *RURALES*
1877 - 1879

Between 1877 and 1879, whilst Papa served as Mr Slaughter's agent in the San Pedro River Valley, I abode with my Neri relatives in Sonora, attending class with my brother Horace at Los Neri. School holidays, however, I almost always spent with Papa in Charleston.

During that period, *rancheros* in northern Mexico suffered devastating losses from cattle rustling. American cowboys raided across the border, ruthlessly shooting down Mexican *vaqueros* in order to steal the herds they tended.

The term *cowboy*, by the way, I am using in the old way to mean a *cattle thief*. This original definition dates back at least as far as the American Revolution, when Tory guerrillas, in order to supply beef to the king's army, would steal oxen from farmers supporting the revolutionary cause. One such marauder, Claudius Smith, known as the *Cowboy of the Ramapos*, was hanged in 1779 at Goshen, New York.

Today, of course, the word *cowboy* has come to mean a *stockman*, a *drover*, or a *herdsman*. Dime novels, identifying Anglo-American *vaqueros* as *cowboys* and glamorizing both the lifestyle and the word itself, are largely responsible, it seems to me, for the term's original meaning to have been lost. Throughout the Borderlands during my childhood, a cowboy was clearly understood to be an outlaw of the worst kind.

The *rurales* made stopping the cowboys' cross-border raiding their number-one priority, but geography was against them. All the rustlers had to do in order to be safe from pursuit was to manage to get back across the frontier before they were overtaken. The *rurales* had no authority to enter the

United States, and the US Army was unable (or unwilling) to be of assistance.

"The army is charged with keeping the Indians on their reservations and tracking down the renegades that do occasionally break out," *tío* Felipe was told by the commandant at Fort Bowie. "Criminal matters in the United States and its territories are the concern of civilian law-enforcement agencies. The army has no authority to act. I suggest you take this issue up with the Pima County Sheriff's Office in Tucson."

This *tío* Felipe would certainly have done had not a more promising solution to his problem presented itself in the person of two deputy US marshals apprehended in Mexico by *rurales* on the lookout for cowboy raiders. John Hicks Adams and Cornelius Finlay stood before *tío* Felipe disarmed, embarrassed, and most likely fearful of incarceration.

"We owe you an abject apology, *comandante*, for violating the sanctity of the border between our two nations," Finlay said, "but we were in hot pursuit of bandits that stole five hundred pounds of silver bullion. We were about to overtake them

45

when your men surrounded us. There simply wasn't time to seek your help."

"You have arrest warrants for these men?" *tío* Felipe asked.

"We do," said Adams, producing the documents.

"And who is your superior? To whom do you report?"

"Crawley Dake is the US marshal for the entire Arizona Territory. His office is in Prescott."

"And you have come all the way from Prescott yourselves?"

The two men nodded. "Yes, *comandante.*"

"As it happens, I can very well appreciate your dilemma, knowing that international law requires you to get permission before entering my country in pursuit of criminals and knowing also that to break off pursuit would mean that your quarry would escape. I am faced with the same problem. American cowboys frequently stage raids on *ranchos* this side of the border, then escape back north before my men can catch up to them. Perhaps we can be of assistance to each other, Marshal Dake and I. What do you think?"

Adams smiled. "*Comandante*, I believe you and Marshal Dake are going to get along famously."

"Leave those warrants with me," *tío* Felipe suggested. "If I am able to apprehend your *desperados*, I'll contact Marshal Dake and he can request extradition. In the meantime, you be sure to inform the marshal about our conversation today, and tell him, please, that I shall be calling on him in Prescott as soon as I can spare a few days away from here."

Unfortunately, Adams and Finlay never made it back to Prescott. On September 2, 1878, they were ambushed in the Arizona wilderness and killed by a party of outlaws, only one of whom— Florentino Saiz—was ever identified. The wanted murderer fled south to Mexico, where he was arrested by the *rurales* and held for extradition. A Mexican *juez*, however, refused to grant that extradition.

Still, *tío* Felipe and Marshal Dake had, by this time, come to a secret agreement whereby either might feel free to cross the border in hot pursuit of violent criminals. The extradition process could then be avoided with a little creativity in writing up arrest reports. Mind you, neither the US Cavalry nor the Mexican *federales* were a party to this agreement. But both those armies were spread so thin in the region as to constitute no real threat to possemen on the wrong side of the frontier.

The following July, a band of cowboys carried out a violent attack on a little *ranchito* quite near to Los Neri. Women and girls were raped, several men were slain, and livestock was stolen. When word of the incident reached Los Neri, *tío* Felipe immediately dispatched a large company of *rurales* under the command of Captain Alfredo Carrillo.

The Peloncillo Mountains are ranged along the border between Arizona Territory and New Mexico Territory and extend south well into Mexico. Within that range is Guadalupe Canyon, known to many Mexicans as *Cañon Bonita* and to some Anglo-American ranchers in the area as *Skeleton Canyon*.

It was through this canyon that the fugitive cowboys made their escape from Mexico. Captain Carrillo and his men were so close behind that they could hear the lowing of the stolen cattle up ahead. Heedless of any danger, the *rurales* entered Guadalupe Canyon at a gallop. Suddenly, shots broke out all around them. The cowboys had concealed themselves in the rocks above the trail. Only three of the *rurales* made it back to Los Neri. All were badly wounded. A much-chagrined Captain Carrillo was one.

The government in Mexico City sent a letter of outrage to President Chester A Arthur. If there was ever any response, I am unaware of it.

Meanwhile, Papa's employment with Mr Slaughter had come to an end. Back in the spring, Mr Slaughter (now age thirty-seven) had re-married at Tularosa, New Mexico Territory. His new bride, Cora Viola Howell, was but eighteen years of age. When the Slaughters arrived in the San Pedro River Valley to occupy their new home, they were accompanied by Viola's parents and by Mr Slaughter's long-time employees, all of whom were as close as family. Some, in fact, were cousins. Mr Slaughter offered Papa the opportunity to remain in his employ, but in the reduced capacity of a range detective. That was work that Papa had done before, but Papa was anxious now to find a new occupation that would not keep him in the saddle and away from home for days at a time.

He returned briefly to Los Neri in order to collect Horace and me, intending to move the three of us to Tombstone. Horace wept and begged to be allowed to remain at Los Neri. He was happy there and terrified of ever again traveling through the wilderness. Reluctantly, Papa agreed. The Neris were overjoyed to have Horace continue to live with them. My grandfather tried to coax me into staying as well, but I was determined, if at all possible, to be wherever my father was.

In late November, Marshal Dake paid an official visit to *tío* Felipe, informing him that he had recently appointed a new deputy to help police the southeast corner of Arizona Territory.

"His name is *Virgil Earp*. He's an experienced lawman. He should be in Tombstone by the first of December. His prime mandate will be to deal with these cowboys. We are now pretty sure that we know who they are. I'll give you a list of those we suspect. Of course, we'll have to gather evidence before we can begin arresting them. I've asked Earp to extend you every courtesy and to cooperate closely with your men."

To Papa, *tío* Felipe later said, "I want you to serve as intermediary between this Deputy Earp and me. You will be returning here from time to time to visit Horace, I presume."

"Yes, of course," Papa agreed. "And I'll be delighted to be your go-between."

"Keep me posted on events on your side of the border. I'd like to get a feel for what this man Earp is like. Can I trust him? Can I depend on him? Is he even honest? I am halfway convinced that many lawmen in Arizona Territory are in collusion with the cowboys."

"Give me a letter of introduction. I'll call on Earp as soon as we arrive in Tombstone. Mind you, that won't be till after the first of the year. Will that be soon enough? Gaby and I want to spend Christmas here with Horace."

CHAPTER VII
Tombstone, Arizona Territory
1880

Horseback, one would ordinarily expect to spend the better part of a day traveling between Los Neri and Tombstone. Papa and I stretched the trip out to three full days. Taking a meandering route, we paused along the trail and spent hours practicing marksmanship each afternoon. Before leaving Los Neri, you see, Papa had presented me with two hand guns to be my own, and he wanted me to get used to using them both before we reached our destination.

The first was a hide-out gun, a brand new Remington Model 95 Derringer (.41 caliber) small enough to carry in my pocket. The second was an old Navy Colt in a new holster and gun-belt (custom-made to fit my slender eleven-year-old figure). The belt was expandable with more holes than belts usually have. Today, at age thirty-one, I can still buckle that same gun-belt around my waist.

That Navy Colt, by the way, was the very weapon that had earned Papa his reputation as a *pistolero* all those years ago down in Durango. He had graduated to Smith and Wesson only after coming north. The Navy Colt, before being relegated to the gun chest, had been modified to fire .38 caliber cartridges. Originally, it had been a cap-and-ball pistol. It fit my hand perfectly. It was well-balanced and not too heavy for me. In almost no time, I was as good with that gun as Papa himself had ever been. At least, that's what he told me, and it suited my pride to believe him.

"In Tombstone," he told me, "you won't be carrying the Colt, but you can keep the Derringer in your pocket. Just remember, it's not a toy. Don't flash it around. Don't let anyone know you have it. It's for the direst of emergencies only. I don't ever want you to be defenseless. And whenever we're on the trail, you can wear the gun-belt as well."

Entering Tombstone, Papa and I were both astride magnificent black horses, which attracted many admiring glances. Papa's mount was a stallion without a trace of white. His name was *Nube de Truenos*, which means *Thunder Cloud*, for that is exactly what he looked like, a thunder cloud, powerful and dangerous. Papa called him *Nube*. My horse, a recent gift from my grandfather, was a fleet but gentle two-year-old gelding with a white blaze on his forehead and one white stocking. I named him *Calcetín*, which is Spanish for *Sock*. The only other horse in Tombstone as impressive, as valuable, or as fast as Nube and Calcetín was a race horse owned by Virgil Earp's younger brother Wyatt.

In Tombstone, we boarded our steeds at the Dexter Livery Stable and took rooms for ourselves at the newly built Cosmopolitan Hotel on Allen Street. Our host was Carl Bilicke. He and his grown son Albert had begun this business the year before in a tent. Even then, the Bilickes had claimed to have the only real beds in Tombstone, other establishments of the like offering only cots.

Within the hotel was a stylishly decorated restaurant. A saloon bar next door was still under construction but due to open in the spring. The Cosmopolitan was easily the most elegant hotel in Tombstone. I was really glad that we did not have to sleep in a tent with other people nearby, as Papa had warned me we might.

Tombstone, although spread out over an area of about nine square miles, was not yet a proper city. The population was perhaps six or seven hundred but would more than double over the next few months and reach seven thousand by the end of the following year.

Out shopping on the day after our arrival, Papa and I ran into Mr Slaughter and his new wife Viola, whom he introduced to us. She was very pretty and seemed quite nice. I liked her instantly.

"My goodness, Gaby!" exclaimed Mr Slaughter. "You certainly have grown. Why, I believe you're taller than I am now."

It was true. I was tall for my age, but then, Mr Slaughter was himself only five feet two inches in height. I did not mention that fact. I simply said, "Thank you," even though I wasn't entirely sure that his observation could really be counted a compliment.

That same day, Papa paid a call on Virgil Earp at his office above the Crystal Palace Saloon. We climbed outside stairs to enter a long, wide hallway from which opened six doors, three on either side. The first door on the left was clearly marked *Deputy US Marshal Virgil Earp*. At Papa's suggestion, I took a seat on a bench just outside that door. Papa knocked and was admitted.

After perhaps ten or fifteen minutes, I began to feel restless. Getting to my feet, I wandered down the hallway to see who else had offices on this floor. Neat gold-and-black lettering on the doors indicated the tenants to be Pima County Coroner Dr HM Matthews, Attorney at Law George W Berry, Justice of the Peace Wells Spicer, and George Goodfellow, MD. The last office was vacant and the door was ajar; so I tiptoed in to look around. I could not possibly have guessed then, but this room would soon be rented to Pima County Sheriff Charles Shibell to serve as the office of a yet-to-be-named deputy for the eastern portion of the county. Sheriff Shibell's own office, of course, was in Tucson, the county seat close to sixty miles away.

"Gaby!" It was Papa's voice, and he sounded quite alarmed. He had finished his business with Deputy Earp and panicked when he didn't find me on the bench where he had left me.

I hurried to exit the empty office and was quick to apologize for having given Papa such a scare.

"As big as you are," he said crossly, "I ought to spank you."

I had never been spanked in my life. Nor had I ever seen Papa so angry. I was genuinely frightened and abjectly contrite. Happily, Papa's ire soon evaporated.

Deputy Earp joined us for lunch that day at Quong Kee's Cancan Chop House. That was my first taste of Chinese food. American cuisine was on the menu too, but I have always been an adventurous eater.   If there is something offered that I have never eaten before, I am eager to try it.

It was in Tombstone, by the way, that I first enjoyed shrimp, crab, and abalone, all shipped in fresh every day from California.

A special election in January made Fred White Tombstone's first town marshal.   He and Virgil Earp then negotiated an arrangement whereby they would share the office above the Crystal Palace.

Marshal White was a genteel young man, friendly with all elements within the community. Party politics in Tombstone was a vicious business, but Marshal White refused to be drawn into the petty power struggles and backstabbing.   He was universally popular.   I was halfway in love with him myself.   Of course, to him, I was just a child.   I knew that I didn't stand a chance with him, but I could hardly help it if my heart gave a little flutter whenever I saw him walk by or heard his name mentioned.

There was not yet a church building in Tombstone, but in 1879, Sacred Heart Parish had been established there.   Whilst money was being raised for the construction of a sanctuary, Father

Antonio Jouvenceau celebrated Mass and heard Confession out of doors. In inclement weather, various merchants, during off hours or on days that they were closed, made space available for religious services inside their places of business. Papa attended as often as he was able. He also arranged for me to start receiving instruction for my first Communion. I didn't want to, but Papa insisted.

In February, a new school was established in Tombstone. I was enrolled and attended class on opening day. Initially, there were only half a dozen other students, their ages ranging from six to sixteen years. By the end of term, there would be more than three dozen scholars in attendance.

Sitting next to me on that first day was Mr Bilicke's thirteen-year-old daughter Louisa, whom I already knew from the hotel, for she helped out on a daily basis, doing whatever odd jobs needed doing. Sometimes, she waited tables in the restaurant; other times, she helped the chambermaids change sheets.

One of those chambermaids, was seventeen-year-old Mary Jane Evans, whom Louisa called *May*. I never understood why. *May* is not a common nickname for *Mary Jane*, is it? In any event, Louisa and May (or Mary Jane, if you prefer) were the very best of friends.

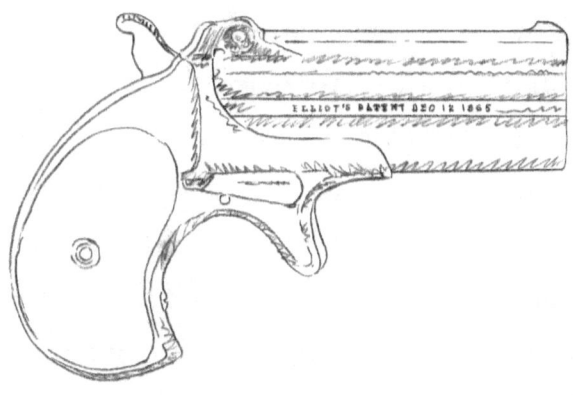

CHAPTER VIII
FRED DODGE
1880

Papa had known Fred Dodge for years. Where they first met and under what circumstances I never heard.

"Durango!" Mr Dodge exclaimed when we chanced to meet him on the street. "It's good to see you. Is this your sprout?"

"Howdy, Fred," said Papa. "Long time no see. Yeah, this is my daughter Gabriela. Gaby, say *hello* to Mr Fred Dodge." Conspiratorially, Papa added, "Fred's a detective for Wells Fargo."

"How do you do, Mr Dodge," said I, offering him my hand to shake.

Mr Dodge replied, "I hope that I can count on your discretion, Gabriela. I shouldn't want it to get about that I'm a detective. There has been a spate of stage-coach robberies lately, and I'm hoping to overhear some little scrap of information that will lead me to discover who the culprits are. Mind you, I already have my suspicions."

"Don't worry, Mr Dodge. I know very well how to keep my mouth shut. In fact, I'm undercover myself, trying to discover the identity of the rustlers that steal cattle in Mexico and drive them back north to sell for beef in Tombstone."

"Gaby," Papa scolded me, "I don't want you poking about in this business. Those cowboys are dangerous. They wouldn't think twice about killing you. You leave the detective business to Fred and me."

"Yes, sir," I said, but behind my back, my fingers were crossed.

I had already proven to my own satisfaction that I could go almost anywhere in Tombstone and not even be noticed. Bars, billiard parlors, and bordellos were off-limits, of course, but hanging out near the entrances, I was almost completely invisible. Grown-ups about their grown-up business simply do not see children. Nor do they appreciate that children hear, see, and remember everything.

Papa offered to share with Mr Dodge the list of suspected rustlers that had been furnished *tío* Felipe by Marshal Dake. "Outlaws are outlaws. Rustlers might well be stage robbers too."

"Absolutely," Mr Dodge agreed. "Let's see what you have."

The list that Papa handed to Mr Dodge consisted of fourteen names:

Newman Clanton & Ike Clanton

Phineas Clanton & Billy Clanton

Pete Spence

Tom McLaury & Frank McLaury

Dick Gray & John P Gray

Curly Bill Brocius & Johnny Ringo

Pony Diehl & Charley Snow

Rattlesnake Bill (last name unknown)

After perusing the list carefully, Mr Dodge folded the paper and handed it back to Papa, saying, "Old Man Clanton—that's *Newman Clanton* on your list—seems to be the mastermind behind a vast and well-organized criminal syndicate. Some of the others on your list are his immediate henchmen. I am already familiar with all those names. Indeed, I have a far more extensive list of my own if you're interested."

"By all means."

In addition to the names on Papa's list, there were eleven names on Mr Dodge's list previously unknown to Papa:

Jim Hughes & Billy Claiborne

Indian Charlie (AKA Florentino Cruz)

Mike Lang & Joe Hill

Billy Grounds & Billy Byers

Jake Gauge & Charles Thomas

Frank Stilwell & Jim Crane

"The Clantons," Mr Dodge informed Papa, "have a second ranch over in New Mexico Territory in the Animas Valley just across the border from Arizona Territory. Their criminal activities are by no means restricted to Arizona Territory and Sonora. Even the Texas Rangers have expressed an interest in bringing them to justice for crimes committed in Texas. So far, though, no one has been able to come up with any rock-solid evidence against them."

As we chatted, we were strolling along Allen Street in the direction of our hotel. From the opposite direction, walking toward us, came four heavily armed men in attire typical of Texas stockmen. Papa and Mr Dodge recognized them all.

"Pony Diehl and Johnny Ringo in front," Mr Dodge said, presumably for my benefit. "Sherman McMaster and Turkey Creek Jack Johnson bringing up the rear."

Because the sidewalk was narrow—just wide enough for two people—both groups (ours and the gunmen's) now strung out single file to pass. Papa stepped ahead of me, and Mr Dodge came behind. The first man we met was Johnny Ringo, who stopped briefly to speak to Papa. I think he meant to taunt him into a gunfight right there in the street, but Papa was having none of it.

"Durango!" Ringo exclaimed in mock surprise. "I thought somebody would have killed you by now. Looks like I may have to do it myself."

Papa's only response was a hard stare straight into the eyes of his old enemy. Ringo laughed heartily and took another step or two, only to pause again beside me.

"You must be Little Durango. You're a heap purtier than your Pa."

He looked me up and down, the way a man appraises a horse he is thinking of buying. I half expected him to force my mouth open so he could examine my teeth. My hand in my pocket was on my Derringer. Had Ringo so much as touched me, I meant to shoot him to preempt Papa's doing so.

"I'll be around to see you in a year or two, darlin', when you've had time to ripen up a bit."

Furious, I spat in his face. He laughed again and walked on by. Pony Diehl and Turkey Creek Jack Johnson passed silently, tipping their hats politely to each of us. As Sherman McMaster came close, Papa said quietly, "You're keeping pretty bad company these days, Sherm."

McMaster bowed his head in shame and muttered under his breath, "*No todo es como parece, amigo.*"

When the four gunmen were beyond earshot, Mr Dodge asked Papa what McMaster had said to him.

"He said that not everything is as it seems."

Forgetting Papa's strict rule that I was never to interrupt a grown-up conversation, I asked, "What do you think he meant by that, Papa?"

I guess Papa didn't notice. Or perhaps he had begun to accept that I was almost grown now. "The last time I crossed paths with Sherman McMaster," he said, "he was a Texas Ranger, a damned good one too. I figure he was letting me know that he's undercover, trying to infiltrate the Clanton Gang."

Mr Dodge nodded. "Whew! That's a dangerous game to be playing. But I reckon you might be right. I pray they don't cotton on to him."

Dining with us that evening at the restaurant in the Cosmopolitan Hotel, Mr Dodge asked Papa whether he might be interested in a job as shotgun messenger. "I'd be pleased to write you a letter of introduction. Marshall Williams, the local agent here, trusts my judgment of men. It was on my recommendation that he hired Wyatt Earp."

"Thanks, Fred," Papa told him, "but I shouldn't feel comfortable leaving Gaby on her own whilst I'm out of town on a run. I'm hoping to find work as a deputy constable or maybe a lookout at one of the gambling houses. I need to be able to work a regular day shift."

Now, before I close this chapter, there's one other interesting fact about Mr Dodge that I should like to mention. He kept a diary and wrote in it almost every day. It was this curious habit of his that inspired me to start keeping a diary of my own. As I compose this narrative, I refer constantly to my old diaries (twenty volumes to date) in order to be certain that I get every detail correct. It is my intention that this personal memoir of mine also be a true account of the taming of the Arizona Borderlands.

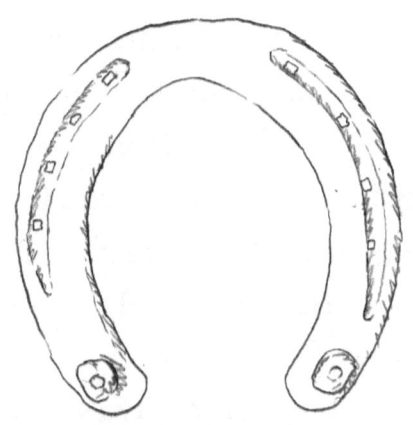

CHAPTER IX
BUCKSKIN FRANK LESLIE
1880

Bars and casinos in Tombstone stayed open twenty-four hours a day seven days a week. Papa, serving as a lookout at the Oriental Saloon, was, therefore, able to work a shift that roughly coincided with my school day. Of course, I got home a couple of hours before he did, but even so, we always managed to enjoy breakfast and supper together, usually at the hotel restaurant. Once or twice a week, we dined at the Cancan or at one of the other upscale eateries.

In any event, it was my habit, after school each weekday, to wait on the front porch of our hotel for Papa to get home from work. Curled up on a wooden bench, I hurried through my homework assignments, then read a chapter or two in the latest Ned Buntline novel.

Glancing up from my book in hopes of seeing Papa walking up the street toward me was how I happened to observe Frank Leslie's arrival in Tombstone. Mind you, I had no idea who he was, but I knew immediately that this was a man of some distinction. As dusty and trail-worn as he was, he exuded an air of quiet self-confidence. He was attired head to toe in buckskins so sweat-stained and dirty that it seemed to me he must have been wearing those same clothes since before I was born. His eyes were icy blue, and he sported the most impressive mustache I have ever seen. When he noticed me staring at him, he tipped his hat and smiled warmly.

I returned his smile and gave him a shy little wave. Mind you, I was careful not to exhibit too much enthusiasm. It wouldn't do to appear overly friendly.

He turned his pony—a brown-and-white pinto —in my direction and came to a halt directly in front of me. My heart was pounding fiercely, so nervous was I. I wasn't afraid that he might do me harm. I could read in his face only friendliness. I suppose that what I must have been anxious about was somehow making a fool of myself or sounding stupid if he asked me a question I couldn't answer.

The great scout—for this is how I had already come to think of him—climbed out of the saddle and tied his pony to a cast-iron hitching post. Then without acknowledging me any further, he strode into the hotel to rent a room.

After a few minutes' hesitation, I followed him in. He had already signed the guest register and paid.

"Excuse me, sir," I said to him. "Want me to take care of your horse? My Papa and I keep ours at Dexter Livery Stable. I can lead yours over there if you want."

"I'd be much obliged, lassie. You can ride him if you prefer. He ain't exactly gentle, but he's way too tired to give you much trouble."

I shook my head emphatically. "No, thank you. I'm all cleaned up and waiting for my Papa to take me to supper. He'll be home any minute now. I don't want to get dirty and stinky."

Laughing, the man slipped me a coin. "What's your name, sugar?"

"*Gabriela Falcón,* but I prefer to be called *Little Durango.*"

"I suppose your Papa must be *Big Durango?* Is that the way of it?"

"Not exactly. Years ago, he was known as the *Durango Kid,* but he hasn't been a kid in decades. That's what he always tells people. Anyway, he just goes by *Durango* these days."

"Well, it's a pleasure to meet you, Little Durango. I'm Frank Leslie. Folks call me *Buckskin Frank.*"

"Oh, my god!" I exclaimed. "You're Frank Leslie. I knew that you must be somebody important. I love your magazine. I read every single issue cover to cover. Do you draw all those pictures yourself?"

Mr Leslie looked totally confused. "My magazine?"

"Frank Leslie's Illustrated Newspaper, I mean. I just called it a magazine because it seems more like a magazine to me than a newspaper."

Mr Leslie laughed heartily. "Sorry to disappoint you, but I'm not that Frank Leslie. I'm just a former army scout in search of a new occupation."

At dinner that evening, I was telling Papa about my having met Tombstone's latest new-arrival when through the restaurant door came the man himself, no longer in dirty old buckskins, but clean, freshly shaven, and smartly attired in city clothes. He could have passed for a senator or a congressman.

"That's the man I was telling you about, Papa. That's Buckskin Frank Leslie. He looks different now. You should have seen him before."

Not many days after that, Mr Leslie, in partnership with William H Knapp, bought the not-yet-finished Cosmopolitan Saloon next door to the hotel. Mr Bilicke, it seemed, had got himself a bit overextended and needed to sell the saloon in order to protect his investment in the hotel and restaurant. Under the management of Leslie and

Knapp, the Cosmopolitan Saloon opened for business a few weeks later.

On opening day, free beer tokens were handed out. Taking full advantage, Johnny Ringo drank a lot more beer than he was used to and began to boast openly and loudly of having ambushed a company of Mexican *rurales* several months earlier.

Outside in the alleyway, beneath the open saloon windows, I happened, at that moment, to be playing jack stones with Louisa Bilicke. My ears pricked up, and I put my finger to my lips to ask for silence in order that I might hear everything that was being said within. And that, Dear Reader, is how I learned the identities of all the cowboys that had participated in the massacre of *tío* Felipe's men the previous summer.

The murderers, according to Johnny Ringo, were himself, the McLaury brothers (Frank and Tom), three of the Clantons (Ike, Billy and their father Newman), Curly Bill Brocius, and Indian Charlie (otherwise known as *Florentino Cruz*). I wondered briefly whether Florentino Cruz might, in fact, be Florentino Saiz, wanted in Prescott for the murder of two deputy US marshals.

I immediately informed Virgil Earp, who questioned several individuals known to have been in attendance all afternoon at the grand opening of the Cosmopolitan Saloon. Deputy Earp was unable to find a single witness willing to testify to having heard what I had heard.

When Papa came in from work later that afternoon, I told him what I had told Mr Earp. Papa then took a few days off from work, and together, he and I rode to Los Neri to inform *tío* Felipe of this latest intelligence.

By the time we got back to Tombstone, Mr Leslie, to complement his fancy city duds, had begun wearing a brand new buckskin jacket with Native American beadwork and long beautiful fringe. Apparently, buckskin was his trademark, just as all-black attire was Papa's.

The chambermaid May Evans had caught Mr Leslie's attention and totally captured his imagination. He flirted with her and teased her and did his best to get her to fall in love with him. But she was already being courted by a man named

Mike Killeen. In fact, she had committed herself to marrying Mr Killeen. The date of their wedding was set.

"Can't we just be friends?" May begged Mr Leslie. "I really like you a lot, but a girl can't be in love with two men at the same time, can she?"

"No, of course not," he said graciously. "I'd be proud for you to count me as a friend."

The wedding of May (Mary Jane) Evans to Mike Killeen took place on April 13, 1880, at the Cosmopolitan Hotel. Louisa Bilicke served as maid of honor, and Buckskin Frank Leslie was first in line to congratulate the groom and to kiss the bride.

FRANK LESLIE'S
ILLUSTRATED
NEWSPAPER

No. 1,109—Vol. XLIII.]

NEW YORK, DECEMBER 30, 1876.

[Price, 10 Cents.

THE BROOKLYN THEATRE CONFLAGRATION.

THE ROOM OF THE PROPERTY CLERK AT THE BROOKLYN POLICE HEADQUARTERS—FRIENDS OF THE MISSING IDENTIFYING RELICS FOUND IN THE RUINS OR ON THE BODIES OF THE VICTIMS.—See Page 279.

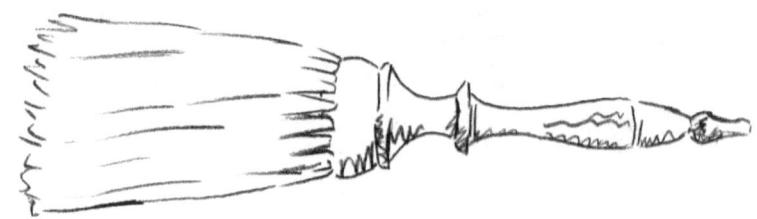

CHAPTER X
ELLEN CASHMAN & JOHN CLUM
1880

The most astonishingly beautiful woman I have ever seen, even in magazines, was Ellen Cashman, known to me as *Miss Nellie*. She arrived in Pima County from British Columbia to open a dry-goods store in Tombstone. Papa (and probably every other man in the region) immediately fell in love with her, for she was ever so kind and always helpful and considerate. In Canada, she had earned the sobriquet *Angel of the Cassiar* for her rôle in saving the lives of several miners stranded in a blizzard. She was already famous when she came to Arizona. I had read all about her heroic deeds in *Frank Leslie's Illustrated Newspaper*.

78

A devout Catholic, Miss Nellie, immediately upon her arrival in Tombstone, set about to help Father Antonio collect money for the first church building to be erected in our town. She was infinitely more adept at fundraising than he had, so far, showed himself to be. And because Papa too was such a devout Catholic, he was allowed to call on her. In Tombstone, Papa was Miss Nellie's only real beau.

Although much younger than Papa himself, Miss Nellie was very nearly old enough to have been the mother of either of Papa's previous wives. I believe Miss Nellie's age, when first we encountered her, was thirty-five or thirty-six years. Papa would certainly have married her had not Fate cruelly intervened. The two seemed made for each other. As for me, I found her easy to love. I should have been delighted to accept her as my stepmother.

Miss Nellie, by the way, had been born across the Atlantic in County Cork and brought to America as a child. Traces of her Irish brogue were still detectable from time to time. She told me once that, at my age, she had found employment in a Boston hotel as a bellhop.

That's what gave me the notion of applying for a similar position at the Cosmopolitan. At first, Mr Bilicke seemed reluctant to hire me, but when I offered to work for gratuities only, he could hardly say *no*. I even paid for my own uniform with money borrowed from Miss Nellie. In less than a month, I was able to repay her in full.

At about that same time, Mr John Philip Clum and his wife Mary—or Mollie, as he called her—arrived in Tombstone from Florence, Arizona Territory. There he had been the editor and publisher of a newspaper called *The Arizona Citizen*. In Tombstone, Mr Clum established *The Tombstone Epitaph*, which presented a much more progressive viewpoint than did the already established *Tombstone Nugget*. Mr Clum's premier issue appeared on Saturday, May 1, 1880.

Soon after the Clums' arrival in Tombstone, it became apparent that Mrs Clum was pregnant. The following December, she would be delivered of a daughter, who would be named *Elizabeth*, but called *Bessie*. Mrs Clum would die within days after giving birth, and her baby would survive for only a few months. But of course, those unhappy events were still months in the future.

Mr Clum, I noted in my diary, was a surprisingly handsome man. At age twenty-nine, he was already completely bald on top; yet, somehow, his baldness did not detract in the least from his good looks. I marveled at how a bald man could be so astonishingly attractive.

I suppose that, whilst I have John Clum on my mind, I ought to recount what I know of his life before coming to Tombstone. He is a very illustrious character. Today, he is a US postal inspector in Alaska Territory. But I was about to tell you about his early life.

At age twenty-three, John Clum was appointed Indian Agent to the Chiricahua Apaches, replacing Tom Jeffords. It was Mr Clum, in 1877, that led a posse of Apache Police to capture Geronimo at Ojo Caliente, New Mexico Territory, after the first of his three breakouts. Shortly thereafter, citing near-impossible relations with the US Army, Mr Clum resigned his post to buy *The Arizona Citizen*, which, at that time, was being published in Tucson. Settling in Florence, he began publishing from there.

In Tombstone, Mr Clum became a good friend to Papa, Fred Dodge, Virgil Earp and his brothers James, Wyatt, and Morgan, Marshall Williams (the Wells Fargo agent), EB Gage (a mine owner), Tom Fitch (attorney at law), Lou Rickabaugh (owner of the gambling concession at the Oriental Saloon), and Wells Spicer (Justice of the Peace). These twelve men—all staunch Republicans with liberal values and progressive attitudes—got together frequently (usually in a back room at the Oriental) to discuss current affairs and to debate local politics. They even established a Vigilance Committee to support officers of the law and to help bring an end to violent crime in Tombstone.

In September, a volunteer fire department was created. Wyatt Earp was elected secretary of Tombstone Engine Company No 1. James Vogan (owner of Vogan's Bowling Alley) became treasurer, and Milt Joyce was made assistant foreman. There were other officers, of course, but their names, I feel certain, would be unfamiliar to you. And anyway, I can no longer remember them myself.

Tombstone Epitaph.

DAILY EDITION—VOL. 1, NO. 34.   TOMBSTONE, ARIZONA, SATURDAY MORNING, AUGUST 21.   CLUM, SORIN & CO.

No PRESS REPORT.

Our readers must not blame the Epitaph for lack of telegraphic news this morning, recent storms having again prostrated the telegraph line. We aim to spare neither time nor expense to give our patrons the latest news, but we can't run a stock against Arizona storms, rails and wash-outs and disorganized telegraphic communication.

An Improvement.

M. Calisher & Co. have finally decided that dirt floors in a progressive town like Tombstone are not exactly the thing, and are putting down a nice board floor in their establishment.

Germania Halle.

Our old friend Charles Rodig has reopened the New York brewery under the name of Germania Halle. He purposes keeping only the best of wines, liquors and cigars, and will make a specialty of German lunches.

What Fools These People Be.

Some party or parties during the past few days, seized with the jumping mania, located several lots on the Vizina ground. If they had taken the trouble to have gone to one of the many dumps on the claim and looked at the splendid ore lying around they would finally conclude that there was nothing in such action.

Work Begun.

Superintendent Emanuel of the Vizina Mine, in conjunction with his partner, Mr. E. P. Fixley, has begun work on their claims, adjoining the Vizina, known as the Comstock and Grasshopper. At a depth of thirty feet the former claim shows a splendid ledge of quartzite, mixed quite freely with chloride ore. Mr. Emanuel has great faith in the claims, and expects to make a splendid show-ing inside of 100 feet.

Large Funeral.

The funeral of the late Reuben Saunders took place yesterday, and so far as we have seen was the largest to date in Tombstone, the procession embracing seven or eight carriages and nearly one hundred and twenty footmen. The deceased came to Tombstone from San Diego some time since, and was about twenty-six years of age. About four weeks since he was taken with a fit while standing in front of Tasker & Pridham's, the effects of which brought on typhoid fever, from which he died. Deceased had been employed in the Tough-nut Mine prior to his illness, and was universally liked for his cheerful and accommodating disposition.

Democratic Primaries.

The primaries for the election of six delegates to attend the Democratic County Convention, in Tucson on the 30th, will take place to-day, the polls opening at Danner & Owens' hall, at 3 o'clock p. m., closing at sundown. We learn that two, and perhaps three, tickets will be in the field, the fight being made on candidates for county offices. Why this is so in face of the fact that Tombstone wants a new county and has have no possible interest in who fills the offices in the old one, is to us a mystery. Among the names mentioned as likely to be chosen as delegates we hear those of Samuel Danner, H. A. Fickas, W. T. Lowry, Theodore E. Farish, A. T. Jones and Jerry Ackerson, who are certainly all representative Democrats and property owners. It ain't any of our fight, but we know one thing, as follows, that if the delegation sent from here insists off the legislative ticket for this or that county officer that to the Republicans, aided by the honest Democrats of this section, will be awarded the credit of county division.

TOMBSTONE DAILY NUGGET.

VOLUME III.   TOMBSTONE, COCHISE COUNTY, ARIZONA, FRIDAY MORNING, APRIL 7, 1882.   NUMBER 1015.

THE DAILY NUGGET.

SAN FRANCISCO AGENCY.

H. C. BAKE,

TERMS OF THE WEEKLY TOMBSTONE NUGGET.

One Year $5.00
Six Months $3.00
Three Months 1.50

RATES OF ADVERTISING.

OFFICIAL DIRECTORY.

To Republicans of Cochise County.

NOTICE.

MEETING NOTICES.

UNION NEWS DEPOT!

Agent for All the Leading Periodicals.

Books and Stationery at the Lowest Rates.

SOL ISRAEL,

Proprietor.

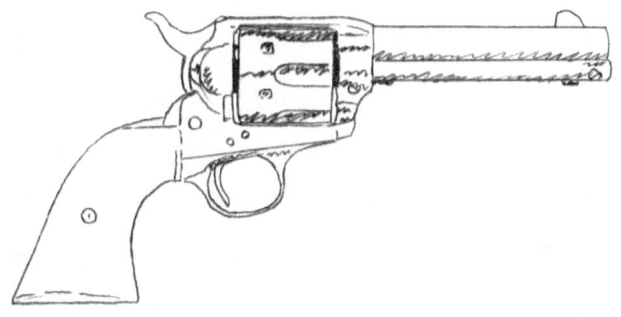

CHAPTER XI
GUNFIGHTS AND SHOOTINGS
1880

The wool uniform I wore as a bellhop was of a deep maroon color with gold piping and a broad gold stripe down each trouser leg. A military-style blouse featured a Mandarin collar and a double row of brass buttons. A chin strap kept a tiny pillbox hat in place on my head at a jaunty angle. I looked very smart. Everyone said so.

"If I weren't so damned afraid of your father," Mr Leslie told me with a wink, "I'd come calling on you. I ain't never in my whole life seen anything cuter than you in that uniform."

On busy days, my tips exceeded the four dollars that a miner was then being paid for his day's labor. Of course, I experienced slow days too and days that I earned nothing at all. But I always had fun. Meeting new people was such a pleasure, and running errands and helping out in other ways made me feel useful. To my thinking, the single greatest satisfaction in life is to feel useful.

Wearing that uniform, I now enjoyed access to saloons, dance halls, billiard parlors, casinos, and even brothels, for I often had to deliver messages to men in those establishments. I wondered sometimes about the lives of the prostitutes and dance-hall girls I saw, many of whom were no more than a year or two older than I was. Of course, I scrupulously avoided mentioning to Papa that I ever had occasion to enter a brothel. He would have made me quit my job, I have no doubt.

I knew by name and by habit just about everyone in Tombstone. I was aware of all the goings-on. Not infrequently was I able to pick up a few extra cents by passing on to Mr Clum some previously unknown detail regarding a local current event that he was covering in his newspaper.

Shootings being commonplace in those days, I had standing orders, whenever the sound of gunfire was heard, to promptly fetch Dr Goodfellow, who was usually to be found at the Crystal Palace Saloon. Only rarely did I have to seek him elsewhere. Once the surgeon had been told of the shooting, I was to notify Marshal White. And if it then transpired that someone had been killed, I was to summon Father Antonio and Dr Matthews, the coroner.

Once, at the scene of a shooting, Dr Goodfellow was examining a wound when one of my school chums, a boy called *Bug* (if I remember correctly) crowded in too close, determined to get a better look at what Dr Goodfellow was doing.

"Son," said Dr Goodfellow good-naturedly, "if you want to treat this man, I'll get out of your way. But if I'm to treat him, you'll have to give me a little room to work."

Dr Goodfellow was (and for that matter, still is) quite an amazing man. A former army surgeon, he pioneered a procedure for treating gunshot wounds to the lower belly, wounds that in the past had been deemed fatal. He has written more than a dozen treatises that have been published in various medical journals around the country.

Dr Goodfellow would eventually serve as coroner for the yet-to-be-created Cochise County, of which Tombstone would be the seat, but that was still several months in the future. In any event, when a man named *McIntire* was killed in a dispute over a card game, Dr Goodfellow was called upon to perform an autopsy. In his report, he wrote that he had performed the "necessary assessment work and found the body full of lead, but too badly punctured to hold whiskey."

Returning now to the spring of 1880, May Evans, upon becoming Mrs Killeen, left her employment at the Cosmopolitan. Mike Killeen was not a man to allow his wife to work. He was, however, a man to beat his wife whenever he happened to be in a foul mood. Ten days after the wedding, May, sporting a black eye, showed up at the hotel asking for her old job back. She and her husband were quits, she explained, and as soon as she could earn enough money to engage a lawyer, she meant to file for divorce.

"Does this mean that I can now hope to be more than just your friend?" asked Mr Leslie.

"Maybe, said May with a flirtatious little smile. "We can talk about it over dinner if you wish."

"I'll be waiting for you when you get off work," Mr Leslie said.

"Somewhere nice," May reminded him.

Throughout that spring, Mr Leslie courted May, escorting her to dances and other social events. He even offered to finance her divorce if she'd just get on with it.

"What's the big hurry, Frank? I'm not going anywhere. Are you?"

Mike Killeen, meanwhile, was boiling with rage. Never mentioning Mr Leslie by name, he swore repeatedly that he'd kill anyone that so much as looked at his wife. Clearly, he still entertained the hope that he might somehow persuade her to come back to him. I could have told him, it wasn't going to happen.

On the evening of June 22, Mr Leslie and May Killeen were sitting together on the same bench where I was wont to read and do my homework.

Out of the darkness came running a frantic George Perine, shouting a warning to Mr Leslie that Mike Killeen was on his way with murder in his heart. Scarcely were the words out of Mr Perine's mouth before two shots rang out, for right behind Perine came Mike Killeen, blind drunk and firing at Frank Leslie. Both bullets grazed Mr Leslie's head, dazing him. By now, Killeen had closed the distance between himself and the object of his hatred. He began beating Mr Leslie about the head with the butt of his pistol. Suddenly, another shot rang out, and Killeen fell to the ground mortally wounded.

In Dr Goodfellow's office, before he died, Killeen swore to witnesses that it had been Mr Perine that had shot him. Marshal White arrested both men (Perine and Leslie). At trial, Mr Leslie testified that he had fired the fatal shot and that he had done so to save his own life. The shooting was, therefore, ruled self-defense, and both defendants were acquitted. I was hugely relieved, for I was inordinately fond of Mr Leslie. As for Mr Perine, I knew almost nothing about him, except that he and Mr Leslie were pals.

A few days after the Killeen shooting, Pima County Sheriff Charles Shibell appointed Wyatt Earp deputy for the entire eastern portion of Pima County. Morgan Earp then stepped into his brother's former position as shotgun messenger for Wells Fargo.

Incidentally, Fred Dodge once told Papa and me that on numerous occasions he had been mistaken for Morgan Earp.

"Yes," Papa agreed. "You and he do look a lot alike. You'd better pray he doesn't have enemies. You could get shot by someone that takes you for him."

"I have enough enemies of my own, thank you all the same."

After a respectable period of mourning—is two weeks usually considered a respectable period of mourning—the young widow May Killeen married again, this time to Frank Leslie, and again Louisa Bilicke served as May's maid of honor. *The Tombstone Epitaph* reported the event as follows:

July 6, 1880, Wedding - Last evening, at 8 o'clock, Mr Nashville Franklyn Leslie was united in holy bonds of matrimony to Mrs

Mary Killeen, (née Evans) by Judge Reilly. The wedding was a quiet one, only a few intimate friends of the parties being present. Miss Bilicke attended the bride, Colonel CF Hines supporting Mr Leslie. There were present during the ceremony, which took place in the parlor of the Cosmopolitan Hotel, Mr and Mrs Bilicke, Colonel HB Jones and wife, Mr CE Hudson and daughter, Miss French, Colonel Hafford, Mr E Nichols, Mr JA Whitcher, Mr Maxon, Mr JA Burres, Mr George E Whitcher, FE Burke, Esq, and Mr Fred Billings. At the conclusion of the ceremony the bridal party and friends repaired to the dining room of the hotel, where a bounteous repast awaited them. *The Epitaph* congratulates Mr Leslie, *un chevalier sans peur et sans reproche*, and his most estimable wife upon this happy event, and earnestly wishes them a pleasant voyage over life's troubled ocean.

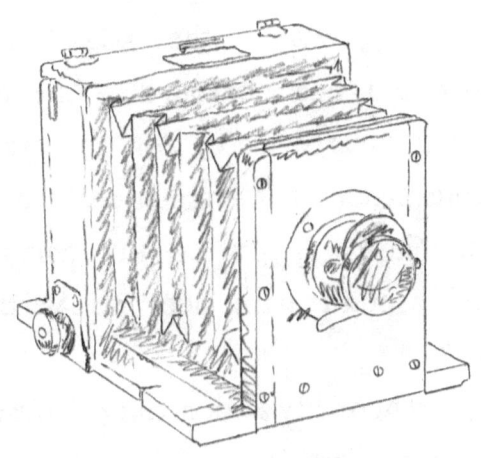

CHAPTER XII

CAMILLUS SIDNEY FLY & JOHNNY BEHAN
1880

Late the previous autumn, a month or so before Papa and I had come to Tombstone, Camillus Sidney Fly, his wife Mollie, and their adopted daughter Kitty had arrived. Mr and Mrs Fly, both of whom were accomplished photographers, had, in December of 1879, established a temporary tent studio. Their portrait business had enjoyed immediate success, and they had soon begun construction of a new studio and a twelve-room boarding house at 312 Fremont Street.

In February, when the school house had opened, Kitty had been enrolled. She and I had not become particularly close, for she was younger than I and conspicuously lacking in maturity. At age eight or nine (just a guess on my part), she still carried a doll around with her and would not be parted from it.

In July, when Fly's Boarding House opened, Doc Holliday was first in line to rent a room. He and Kate Horony, Doc's Hungarian-born wife by common law, had been staying at Deacon Cox's Boarding House, but whenever the couple were feuding, as they were now, they simply could not live together. Of course, it would not be long before they would kiss and make up. Then Kate would move from Cox's to join Doc at Fly's.

Dr John H Holliday had once been a dentist, and he still practiced occasionally, but mostly, he just played cards and drank whiskey. His reputation was that of a quick-tempered gunfighter with a streak of meanness. I never observed any behavior in him to support such notoriety. With me, in fact, he was always extremely polite—deferential even—addressing me as *Miss Falcón*, never by my given name or a nickname and certainly not by any inappropriate term of endearment, such as other men were given to using with me. In fact, I should venture to say that Doc Holliday consistently employed the most polished manners of any man in Tombstone.

I met him first on the day he had his portrait made at the new studio immediately behind Fly's Boarding House. Papa and I were at the studio for the same purpose. When Mr Fly finished taking Dr Holliday's picture, the two men strolled off together in deep conversation. Mrs Fly then took over and showed us into the studio.

The price for a cabinet-card portrait, she told us, was thirty-five cents. We had only a dollar between us, and we wanted three separate images: one of me alone, one of Papa alone, and one of the two of us together.

"I'll do three for a dollar," she said, "but don't you dare tell anyone. If it ever gets back to Buck, I'll be in big trouble."

Buck was what everyone called Mr Fly. We knew that Mrs Fly was joking about being in trouble if her husband found out that she was giving unauthorized discounts. His was the only name on the sign out front, but she was the one that kept the books and managed the business end of things. Any decision she made would never be challenged by him.

On July 25, a Captain Hurst called on Marshal Earp to ask his assistance in recovering six army mules that had been stolen from Camp Rucker. The thieves were three in number, one of whom, based on descriptions given by witnesses, was Curly Bill Brocius.

"We tracked them as far as Babacomari Creek before losing their trail," the young officer explained. "I was hoping you might have an idea where to look."

"Indeed I do," said Marshal Earp. "The McLaury brothers have a little ranch not far from there, and they are known to trade in stolen livestock. How many men do you have with you?"

"Four."

"That's not enough. I'll deputize a few more, and we can be on our way right after lunch."

Marshal Earp enlisted the aid of his brothers Wyatt and Morgan and Wells Fargo agent Marshall Williams. That made a posse of nine.

At the McLaury Ranch (not their main ranch at Soldier's Hole but a second property northwest of Tombstone), the stolen mules were found in a corral. Their brands had been changed from US to D8. A running iron was found in the barn. Marshal Earp was in the process of putting irons on Frank McLaury when a large party of known cowboys led by Frank Patterson showed up. Tom McLaury was with them.

The posse was now outnumbered, but only by half a dozen or so. Marshal Earp did not consider those to be overwhelming odds. He was determined to make the arrest, whatever the cost. Captain Hurst, on the other hand, could not bear to risk the lives of his four young soldiers for the sake of six mules. He persuaded Marshal Earp to let the matter drop.

Back in Tombstone, however, Captain Hurst ordered the printing and distribution of handbills identifying Frank McLaury as a receiver of stolen livestock. He also ran a similar notice in the *Tombstone Epitaph*.

Frank McLaury was livid. It was not, however, toward Captain Hurst that his anger was directed. Instead, he blamed Virgil Earp. He threatened, in front of several witnesses, to kill him if he ever came "snooping around again."

"If you try to kill me, Frank," said Marshal Earp, "it'll be the last thing you ever do."

Later that summer—early September, I believe it was—John Harris Behan, whom everyone called *Johnny*, arrived in Tombstone to manage the saloon at the newly opened Grand Hotel. That barroom, almost directly across the street from the Cosmopolitan, very quickly became the favorite haunt of the worst elements in Tombstone, including all the suspected outlaws on Mr Dodge's list.

Doc Holliday's wife, Kate Horony, also found employment at the Grand Hotel. Of what her job consisted I am not exactly sure.

Johnny Behan, in partnership with John Dunbar, then bought an interest in the Dexter Livery Stable, where Papa and I kept our horses. Initially, I found Mr Behan quite charming and very attractive. Only later did it become apparent to me that he was a man without character or integrity.

With Mr Behan lived his son Albert, who now attended school with me. Albert was such a sweet child (and pitifully unhappy) that, even though he was younger than I was, I felt compelled to befriend him. He confided to me once that he missed his mother and his sister terribly.

Apparently, when his parents had divorced, his father had insisted on Albert's staying with him. Albert's sister was with their mother. Mr Behan, it seemed, was not very fond of his daughter, even going so far as to deny that she was his child.

In October, a former ladyfriend of Mr Behan's came all the way from California to be reunited with him. With money furnished by her parents, she had a house custom-built. Then Albert and his father moved in with her. This lady's name was *Josephine Marcus*, but in Tombstone, she was known as *Mrs Sadie Behan*. Rather than resenting his new step-mother, Albert quite adored her. His own father, on the other hand, he despised.

In the same month that Mrs Behan arrived in Tombstone, I witnessed a gunfight in Milt Joyce's Oriental Saloon. I had been sent there by Mr Bilicke to deliver a message to Mr Joyce. I had just handed over a sealed envelope and accepted a coin in appreciation when Doc Holliday entered the saloon in a blind fury and demanded that Mr Joyce return his pistol. Mr Joyce reached beneath the bar and came out with single-action Colt, but instead of turning it over butt first, he pointed it at Holliday, who instantly produced a double-action revolver and shot Joyce in the hand, disarming him. It was the slickest bit of gun play I have ever seen.

Before the smoke could clear, Mr Joyce's business partner William Parker came running from a back room to join the fight. Doc shot him in the foot, taking off his big toe. A moment later, someone clubbed Doc over the head. I never saw who did that, for my eyes were glued to Mr Parker's bloody boot.

Marshal White arrived seconds later to find Doc Holiday unconscious on the saloon floor. Enlisting the aid of two bystanders, he hauled Doc to jail and charged him with assault and battery.

Doc later pled guilty and paid a hefty fine.

Milt Joyce, I have no doubt, began that very day plotting his revenge. As for how Mr Joyce had come to be in possession of Doc's gun in the first place, I never learned. Nor can I say whether Doc ever recovered it.

On October 28—I shall never forget that date —a terrible tragedy occurred. Curly Bill Brocius shot and killed Fred White, our town marshal. Deputy Sheriff Wyatt Earp arrested Brocius and charged him with murder. So popular had been Marshal White and so disliked was Brocius that talk of a lynching quickly spread about the town. With the help of George Collins, Deputy Earp hurriedly whisked his prisoner away to Tucson and turned him over to Sheriff Shibell.

At trial, Brocius was found *not guilty*, for with his dying breath, Marshal White had assured Dr Goodfellow and others gathered at his bedside that Brocius had not intended to shoot him, that Brocius's gun had gone off accidentally. I myself was not a witness to the event, so I cannot say with any degree of certainty, but I have always doubted that the shooting was indeed an accident. Curly Bill Brocius was a mean, low-down skunk capable of any wickedness that one can imagine. On the other hand, he had always seemed to be on friendly terms with Marshal White.

Two days after the shooting of Marshal White, Virgil Earp was appointed acting city marshal, retaining his commission as deputy US marshal. But when an election was held, Ben Sippy replaced Virgil Earp as city marshal.

CHAPTER XIII
A DISPUTED ELECTION
1880

The November election of 1880 pitted incumbent Democrat Charles Shibell against Republican Robert Paul for the office of Sheriff of Pima County. Paul was strongly favored, but when the votes were counted, it seemed as though Shibell had won.

Allegations of voter fraud were made when various irregularities were uncovered. One precinct in particular had delivered more votes for Shibell than the total number of registered voters in that precinct. Eventually, the election would be overturned, but in the meantime, Shibell remained in office for several weeks whilst the court battle played out. Phineas Clanton, Johnny Ringo, and others were implicated in election wrongdoing but never prosecuted.

Wyatt Earp, who had campaigned vigorously for Robert Paul, resigned as deputy for the eastern portion of Pima County. Papa figured that Sheriff Shibell had likely demanded Wyatt Earp's resignation. But who can say for sure? In any event, Sheriff Shibell then appointed fellow Democrat Johnny Behan to replace Wyatt Earp, who now found employment at the Oriental Saloon.

You will recall that the Oriental Saloon is where Papa was working in those days. Each afternoon, when Papa finished his shift, it would thenceforth be Wyatt Earp that relieved him. At some point—I'm not exactly sure when—Wyatt would buy an interest in the gambling concession at that saloon and thus become Papa's employer (in partnership with Lou Rickabaugh).

On December 18, Joseph Pascholy opened on Toughnut Street at the corner of Fifth Street a hotel and restaurant called *Russ House*. I mention this only because Miss Nellie would eventually become part owner of this establishment.

Now, before I move on to the events of 1881, I must not fail to mention some of the new towns that came into being in eastern Pima County during the year 1880. One of those towns was Maley in the Sulphur Springs Valley, way out near Henry Hooker's Sierra Bonita Ranch. Maley was established by the Southern Pacific Railroad as a whistle stop at the halfway point between El Paso and Phoenix.

Another new town was Benson, which happens to be near to where the Southern Pacific Railroad coming east from California crosses the San Pedro River. When Benson became the nearest railhead to Tombstone, stagecoaches began carrying passengers between those two towns. Benson is about twenty miles to the northwest of

Tombstone. Tucson is another forty-five miles to the northwest of Benson.

Incidentally, in 1882, a railroad station would be built at Junction City (only eight or nine miles from Tombstone), and Benson would no longer be the nearest railhead to Tombstone. Junction City would later be re-named *Kendall*, then *Fairbank.*

Easily the most important new town in southern Arizona Territory was Bisbee, established near the tiny settlement of Don Luis. Bisbee is located twenty-six miles south of Tombstone, only eleven miles from the Mexican border, and ninety-two miles from Tucson. Gold, silver, copper, and turquoise are all mined at Bisbee.

CHAPTER XIV
JOHNNY-BEHIND-THE-DEUCE
1881

Sacred Heart Church, a small adobe structure featuring sanctuary below and rectory above, was dedicated on New Year's Day, 1881. Papa, Miss Nellie, and I attended the service together. I was ever so proud when Miss Nellie received special recognition for her work in raising the money to build this the first church building in Tombstone.

Seeing Miss Nellie home after the services, Papa held her hand, and I walked behind. I wasn't paying much attention to their conversation until I heard the name *Dick Naylor*. Then my ears pricked up, for that was how Wyatt Earp called his race horse.

"And nobody knows who took him?" Miss Nellie asked.

"Papa!" I spoke up loudly. "Did I hear you say that Dick Naylor has been stolen?"

"Missing and presumed stolen," Papa clarified. "He might have broken loose and run away. No one seems to know what happened to him."

"I do," I said. "Or at least, I think I do. I saw Billy Clanton riding him the morning we had such thick fog. I was on my way to Dexter's to check on Calcetín and Nube, and Billy Clanton nearly ran me down in the street. He was riding Dick Naylor at a gallop. I thought it odd, but somehow, it never even occurred to me that anybody would be stupid enough to steal a horse belonging to Wyatt Earp."

"Billy's none too bright," Papa agreed.

Later that day, we called on the Earps at home. The Earp brothers owned a cluster of houses at the corner of Fremont and First Streets, just past the Mexican Quarter. Their closest neighbor was Pete Spence, the former outlaw from Goliad, Texas.

In any event, Mr Earp was mighty grateful to learn what had befallen his horse. "I owe you a big favor, Gaby. I shan't forget this."

Of course, knowing where the horse was and getting it back were two different matters. At the Clanton Ranch might be as many as twenty or thirty cowboys. And Old Man Clanton was in tight with Deputy Sheriff Behan.

Wyatt Earp decided to try a bluff first. He rode to Charleston, looked up Ike Clanton, and told him that, several witnesses having seen Billy ride out of Tombstone on Dick Naylor, Johnny Behan now had little choice but to arrest Billy. "A warrant has been issued, and Johnny's raising a posse now. When that posse descends on the ranch, casualties will be heavy on both sides. To prevent bloodshed, I am prepared to withdraw my complaint against your brother, but in return, I want my horse back."

Ike nodded his acquiescence. "I'll fetch him if you'll wait here. That little brother of mine is a damned fool."

A scant two weeks after that, a shooting in Charleston very nearly provoked a lynching in Tombstone.

Johnny-Behind-the-Deuce was a professional gambler whose birth name, according to the *Tombstone Epitaph*, was *Michael O'Rourke*. On January 14 in the town of Charleston, Johnny-Behind-the-Deuce, defending himself against a knife attack, shot and killed a well-liked mine engineer named *Henry Schneider*. Johnny-Behind-the-Deuce himself was not very popular. It seems that he always—but always—won at cards. He was suspected of cheating, but so far, no one had been able to catch him at it.

Constable George McKelvey arrested Johnny-Behind-the-Deuce, and when talk of a "necktie party" began to circulate, Constable McKelvey put his prisoner in a wagon and struck out for

Tombstone, ten miles away. It wasn't long before a lynch mob formed and set out in pursuit.

Arriving at the outskirts of Tombstone just ahead of the mob, the constable was relieved to encounter Deputy US Marshal Virgil Earp on the road exercising his brother Wyatt's race horse, recently recovered from the Clanton Ranch. Virgil took charge of the prisoner and enlisted the aid of his brother Morgan, who commandeered Vogan's Bowling Alley to serve as a temporary jail. Solid brick and windowless, Vogan's Bowling Alley was deemed the most defensible building in Tombstone.

As soon as City Marshal Ben Sippy and Deputy Sheriff Johnny Behan could be located, those two assumed responsibility for organizing a posse to escort the prisoner to Tucson. Papa and Wyatt Earp were both deputized, as were Buck Fly and his brother Webster Fly, Fred Dodge, Origen Charles Smith (a mine owner known as *Harelip Charlie*), and twelve or fifteen others.

Meanwhile, the lynch mob arrived from Charleston and swelled even greater as Tombstone miners joined the ranks of those demanding instant justice for the slain mine engineer Henry Schneider.

The *Tombstone Epitaph* thus described the confrontation that ensued:

In a few minutes, Allen Street was jammed with an excited crowd, rapidly augmented by scores from all directions. By this time Marshal Sippy...had secured a well-armed posse of over a score of men to prevent any attempt on the part of the crowd to lynch the prisoner; but feeling that no guard would be strong enough to resist a justly enraged public long, procured a light wagon in which the prisoner was placed, guarded by himself, Virgil Earp, and Deputy Sheriff Behan, assisted by a strong posse well-armed. Moving down the street, closely followed by the throng, a halt was made and rifles leveled on the advancing citizens, several of whom were armed with rifles and shotguns.

The wagon with the prisoner, the posse of lawmen, and the angry mob came to a stop directly in front of the Cosmopolitan Hotel. Sitting on the front porch, I was fully convinced that a general melee was about to break out. I was terrified for Papa's safety. Seeing me there, he motioned me to go back inside. I did so, but I continued to watch the goings-on in the street from the lobby windows. I saw and heard everything.

Marshal Sippy calmly addressed the crowd. He was sympathetic to their feelings, he said. He understood full well that they were still angry about Curly Bill Brocius's acquittal, but lynch law was no better than lawlessness, he insisted. He talked and talked and talked and talked. I cannot even remember half of what he said. But little by little, tempers cooled. Eventually the wagon was allowed to pass. The prisoner was put on a train at Benson and delivered the following morning to the Tucson jail, there to await trail.

On April 18, Johnny-Behind-the-Deuce would manage somehow to escape. A few weeks later, it would be reported in the *Tombstone Epitaph* that he had recently been seen in the Dragoon Mountains north of Tombstone:

> He was well mounted and equipped, and was on the eve of departure for Texas. The climate of Arizona, he said, did not agree with him.

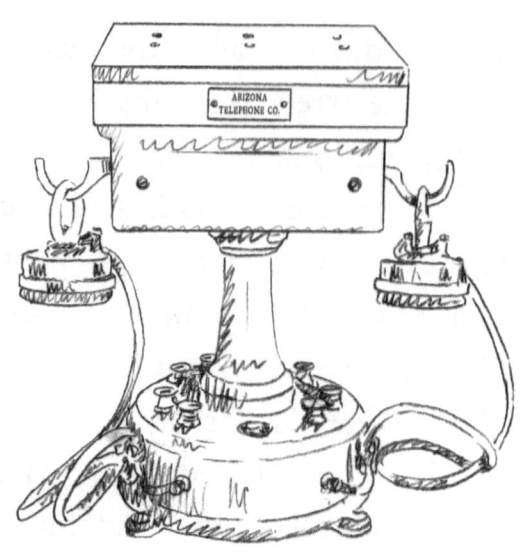

CHAPTER XV
COCHISE COUNTY
1881

On February 1, Cochise County was established from the eastern portion of Pima County. Tombstone was made the county seat. Johnny Behan was appointed sheriff. He had promised Wyatt Earp the position of undersheriff, but changed his mind and gave the job to fellow Democrat Harry Woods instead. Mr Woods was the editor and publisher of the *Tombstone Nugget*.

Now, I suppose, would be as good a time as any to tell you a little about the political climate of the newly formed Cochise County. The more progressive Republican Party tended to represent the interests of mine-owners, business-owners, and townspeople. As mentioned before, the Earps, Mayor Clum, Judge Spicer, and Fred Dodge were all prominent Republicans.

The Democratic Party primarily represented the interests of farmers, ranchers, and herdsmen, most of whom were Southerners still smarting from the defeat of the Confederacy in the Civil War. Mind you, there were a few ranchers and stockmen that voted Republican, just as there were business-owners in Tombstone that were Democrats.

To complicate matters even more, the local Democratic Party was dominated by a corrupt cabal known as the *Ten Percent Ring*, Tombstone's own version of Tammany Hall. Sheriff Behan and Undersheriff Woods were both members of the Ten Percent Ring, within which Old Man Clanton wielded the power of Boss Tweed.

In February of 1881, telegraph service was extended to Tombstone. A month later, telephone poles would begin to be set in place around town and telephone lines strung. Water mains were being laid throughout the town. Fire hydrants were to be installed at every intersection. Tombstone was becoming a proper city, sure enough.

On Friday, February 25, Papa witnessed a gunfight at the Oriental Saloon. He was standing beside the lookout's chair chatting with Wyatt Earp, who had relieved him but moments before. Dealing Faro was Luke Short, newly arrived in Tombstone from the mining camps of Colorado. Nearby were Dr Goodfellow and Bat Masterson, a former lawman from Dodge City.

Charlie Storms, who had earlier quarreled with Short, entered the saloon and approached the faro table. Saying nothing, Storms went for his gun. Short drew and fired twice, killing Storms instantly, and in the process, setting his shirt on fire. That's how close the two men were to each other.

Marshal Sippy arrested Luke Short, but a preliminary hearing determined that the shooting had been in self-defense.

Meanwhile, my school chum Albert Behan experienced great difficulty hearing in class. Early in the year, his step-mother Sadie took him all the way to California to be seen by a specialist. Upon their return a few weeks later, they walked in on Sheriff Behan in bed with another woman. Furious, Sadie demanded that he immediately move out of her house. Such a public breakup was a huge embarrassment to the sheriff and a significant blow to his electability in future elections.

For a while, Albert was allowed to remain with his step-mother, but eventually Sheriff Behan required that his son come to live with him.

On March 15 at ten o'clock in the evening, on the Benson road near Contention City, three masked men attempted to rob a Kinner and Company stagecoach carrying twenty-six thousand dollars' worth of silver bullion. Gunfire was exchanged. One of the would-be robbers was wounded and two people on the coach were killed: driver Eli Philpot (known as *Budd*) and passenger Peter Roerig. Shotgun guard Robert Paul (soon to become the sheriff of Pima County) brought the stagecoach in, and a posse was organized to go after the perpetrators. That posse consisted of the Earp brothers (Virgil, Morgan, and Wyatt), Bat Masterson, Marshall Williams (the Wells Fargo agent), Robert Paul (the future sheriff of Pima County), and Cochise County Sheriff Behan.

Even without an expert tracker, the lawmen found reading sign at the site of the attempted robbery simple enough. Clearly, a fourth member of the gang had held the horses of the three that had stood in the road in an attempt to stop the stagecoach. Tracks led to a small ranch, where the posse found only one man, an out-of-work stockman named *Luther King*. Tracks of the other three led away from the ranch.

King admitted to having held the horses, but refused to name his confederates.

Virgil Earp shrugged, as though the matter was of no great concern to him, then he made up the most outrageous lie. "Suit yourself, King, but I shouldn't want to be in your boots when Doc Holliday directs all his fury against you alone."

"What are you talking about? Why would Doc Holliday have anything against me?"

"Big-Nose Kate was on that stage. She's dead, and she was Doc's woman."

Big-Nose Kate was how some folks spoke of Kate Horony. I cannot think why. Her nose didn't seem all that big to me. Maybe she had a habit of putting it where it didn't belong. But then, I never noticed that about her either.

"I didn't shoot her," King objected. "I didn't even have a gun. I just held the horses."

"You be sure and tell that to Doc Holliday when he comes to visit you in jail."

"Oh, god! Oh, god! What have I got myself into?"

"Perhaps," said Virgil, "if we could bring in the other three, then Doc's ire would be directed at them, instead of you. They're the ones that actually did the crime, are they not?"

"Okay, alright. I'll tell you. It was Harry the Kid Head, Bill Leonard, and Jim Crane. I don't know where they've gone though. They didn't tell me. And that's the truth, so help me God."

"One of them was wounded. Which one?"

"Bill Leonard."

"How bad is he hurt?"

"Hard to say. He was hit in the groin. At first we thought it might be fatal, but once the bleeding stopped, he seemed to be recovering pretty well."

Sheriff Behan and Marshall Williams left the posse to take the prisoner back to Tombstone. Unfortunately, King managed a miraculous escape only minutes after being incarcerated. Someone, it seems, had carelessly left the back door of the jail open. Residents of Tombstone were outraged at such incompetence (if not connivance) on the part of the sheriff and undersheriff.

The rest of the posse continued pursuit of the other three outlaws. The chase took them over four hundred miles and lasted seventeen days. On April 1, they returned to Tombstone afoot and empty-handed. One of their horses had died, and the others were too spent to ride. The men themselves had been without food for three whole days and without water for thirty-six hours.

Sheriff Behan was compensated by the county almost eight hundred dollars for posse expenses but refused to pass any of that money along to the other possemen. The Earps were furious at him.

The fact that Behan had allowed the prisoner King to escape so easily only added to their anger.

Not many days after the return of the posse, Bat Masterson received an urgent telegram and hurriedly left town to return to Dodge City.

As it happens, Doc Holliday and Kate Horony were, at that time, having one of their frequent domestic disputes. Sheriff Behan and Milt Joyce (a county supervisor and owner of the Oriental Saloon) feigned sympathy with Kate for the perceived injustice she suffered at the hands of her common-law husband. Plying her with strong drink, they suggested a sneaky way for her to get even. And so it was that she signed a paper implicating Doc Holliday in the failed stagecoach robbery.

Deputy US Marshal Virgil Earp, however, was easily able to verify Doc's actual whereabouts on the night of the robbery. Dozens of witnesses were willing to swear that Doc had been in Tombstone playing cards and drinking heavily all night long. Judge Spicer ordered that Holliday be set free.

Immediately upon his release, Dr Holliday bought Kate a ticket for Globe City and put her on a stagecoach. He wanted nothing more to do with her, he said. To my thinking, she got off pretty easy.

That same month (April), our city council enacted an ordinance against the carrying of any type of deadly weapon (including firearms and Bowie knives) within the city limits of Tombstone.

On May 25, a shooting occurred at Galeyville, a mining town on the eastern edge of Cochise County, a full day's ride from Tombstone. Curly Bill Brocius was wounded in the neck and face by Jim Wallace, who was then arrested by Deputy Sheriff Billy Breckenridge. At trial, Wallace was acquitted. He probably would have been awarded a medal had he managed to kill Brocius.

On June 6, Marshal Ben Sippy asked the city council for a two-week leave of absence. He had personal business that would take him far from Tombstone, he explained. Virgil Earp was appointed acting city marshal to serve until Sippy's return.

On June 22, Sippy was still away. Around noon, a fire broke out at the Arcade Saloon in the four-hundred block of Allen Street. A bartender was attempting to measure how much whiskey was left in a barrel when fumes escaping from the bung hole were ignited by his cigar. In a matter of minutes, the building was a total loss and other buildings nearby were in flames as well. The fire spread rapidly eastward, consuming sixty-six stores, restaurants, saloons, and office buildings.

Tombstone Engine Company Number 1 was ill-equipped to deal with such a massive conflagration. The fire had simply to be allowed to burn itself out. It took more than six hours to do so.

Virgil Earp deputized Papa, Texas Jack Vermillion, and several others to help keep order and prevent opportunistic looting during the emergency.

Spared from the flames were the Cosmopolitan Hotel and Saloon, Quong Kee's Cancan Chop House, the Occidental Hotel and Saloon, the Grand Hotel, the Alhambra, Campbell and Hatch's Saloon and Billiard Parlor, the entire

Chinese Quarter (called *Hop Town*), the Mexican Quarter, the OK Corral, Dexter Livery Stable, and all else on the west end of Allen Street. Papa, concerned that the wind might shift, had me take our horses well beyond the edge of town and wait there until the danger was past.

Remarkably, as extensive as the destruction was, rebuilding would require but three months.

Ben Sippy, by the way, did not return to Tombstone. During his absence, fiscal irregularities in his department were uncovered. Virgil Earp was, therefore, made Sippy's permanent replacement as city marshal (or chief of police).

Virgil's younger brother Wyatt, meanwhile, had decided to run for sheriff in the next election, which would be held in November of 1882. To enhance his reputation as a lawman, he made it his mission to capture the outlaws Jim Crane, Harry the Kid Head, and Bill Leonard and to recapture their accomplice Luther King. Toward that end, Wyatt asked Papa to set up a clandestine meeting between Ike Clanton and himself. That meeting took place on June 2 in Papa's hotel room. From my room next to Papa's, Papa and I could hardly help overhearing what was discussed.

Citing the Bisbee stagecoach robbery, Wyatt Earp said, "I know that you know those men, Ike. They've been seen often enough in your company."

"So what? That don't mean I'm in cahoots with them."

"No, it doesn't. But I'm thinking that, at some point, you'll hear from them again. I want the credit for bringing them in. Pass any information you have on to me, and I'll see that you get the reward money."

"All of it?"

"Every last penny."

Wells Fargo had offered twelve hundred dollars each for Crane, Head, and Leonard, dead or alive. Apparently, King was too low a priority to justify a bounty.

"If I help you," Ike asked, "can I trust you to keep this under your hat?"

"You have my word on it."

"Alright, I'll see what I can learn. But if this ever gets back to Paw, he'll skin me alive."

"Ike," Earp reassured him, "this is just between you and me."

Later that summer, Doc Holliday and Ike would quarrel over some trivial issue, and Doc would call Ike a "double-dealer." Ike, jumping to the conclusion that Doc had been made privy to the secret arrangement between himself and Wyatt Earp, would become enraged. From that very moment, Ike would be Wyatt's deadly enemy.

On June 8, a theater building called *Schieffelin Hall* was dedicated at the corner of Fourth and Fremont Streets. The theater accommodated four hundred fifty on the main floor and a hundred twenty-five more in the gallery. In that same building was a Masonic Hall of which Judge Spicer was Grand Master.

On September 15, Papa, Miss Nellie, and I should attend a play at Schieffelin Hall. *The Ticket-of-Leave Man* by British playwright Tom Taylor was about a man let out of prison. It was performed by a traveling theatrical troupe.

CHAPTER XVI
Cowboy Comeuppance
1881

In Washington, DC, on July 2, 1881, an attempt was made on the life of the President of the United States, James Abram Garfield. The story appeared on the front page of every newspaper in the country. I was absolutely horrified, for in my lifetime, no such despicable act had ever before occurred. Of course, Papa still clearly remembered the assassination of President Lincoln, a historical event of which I was aware but only in the way that I was aware of the fall of the Roman Empire.

President Garfield, I read, was shot by a former supporter Charles Julius Guiteau, a lawyer angry at having been passed over for a consulship. Initially, it appeared that the President might recover. Vigils and prayer meetings were held at churches throughout the nation but to no avail. Two and a half months after the shooting, President Garfield would succumb to complications from his wound. The following year, Guiteau would face execution by hanging.

The same month that President Garfield was shot, Bill Leonard and Harry the Kid Head attempted an armed robbery in the little mining town of Hachita in the southwest corner of New Mexico Territory. Here the Haslett brothers, William and Isaac, ran a general store. Entering the Haslett General Store with guns drawn, Leonard and Head demanded money. Each got a bellyful of lead instead. That outcome seemed only just to me.

Someone else was of a different mind, for a few weeks later the heroic Haslett brothers were found shot to death. Insomuch as no money was taken from them, this double murder appeared to be an act of vengeance.

I am about ninety-nine percent certain that Johnny Ringo and Pony Diehl were the killers. They and Curly Bill Brocius had been *compañeros* of Head, Leonard, and Crane. All six were members of the Clanton Gang. Brocius too might have participated in this heinous deed had he not been recovering from gunshot wounds received a few weeks earlier. I cannot imagine that he would have felt up to it.

On the other hand, Brocius was positively identified to *tío* Felipe as being one of the twenty or so participants in a second Guadalupe Canyon massacre that occurred later the same month. The victims this time were a group of Mexican smugglers. Four men were killed outright; five escaped to report the ambush. Johnny Ringo was also identified as one of the attackers.

I was still working as a bellhop at the Cosmopolitan Hotel, but I was rapidly outgrowing my uniform. Twice already, I had had to let it out. Soon, I'd have to decide whether to buy myself a new uniform or quit the job altogether.

In the meantime, I managed to overhear a conversation that seemed to implicate a few others in this latest ambush at Guadalupe Canyon. I told Papa, but not Marshal Earp, that I had reason to believe that Jim Crane, Jake Gauge, Charles Thomas, Billy Grounds, and Joe Hill had been active participants in that ambush.

"Just keep it to yourself," Papa advised me. "I'll pass it along to Felipe, but the law on this side of the border can't do anything without a witness deemed more reliable than you. And no one in Tombstone is going to risk his life by testifying against any associate of Old Man Clanton."

"I'm completely reliable," I objected.

"Not in the eyes of the legal system. In the first place, you're Mexican. In the second place, you're female. And finally, you're only twelve years old."

"Twelve and a half," I corrected him.

"No American court is going to convict on the weight of a conversation you alone claim to have overheard."

"I did overhear it, Papa."

"I know, Gaby. And a day of reckoning is coming for these cowboys. Just continue to keep your ears open, but never—and I mean never—let on that you're paying the least bit of attention to what's being said around you."

"That's exactly what I do, Papa. They hardly even notice that I'm present."

In early August, we got the break we had been waiting for. A large herd of cattle stolen in Mexico and being held at Clanton's ranch in the Animas Valley, I learned, was soon to be driven to Clanton's ranch in the San Pedro River Valley. The route of the trail drive was to be through Guadalupe Canyon. I even knew the departure date. I told Papa immediately, and we each took a leave of absence and rode to Los Neri to inform *tío* Felipe. Now it was our turn to bushwhack the bushwhackers.

Unfortunately, I was not allowed to participate. Captain Carrillo led the expedition with Papa as his scout. On the night of August 12, the *rurales* silently surrounded the sleeping cowboys where they had camped for the night inside the canyon. At daybreak, Old Man Clanton was the first to rise. He stirred the fire to life and began making breakfast. Most of the cowboys were still in their bedrolls. When the *rurales* opened fire, Old Man

Clanton fell dead face down in the campfire. Only one man—Harry Ernshaw—managed to escape into the wilderness unscathed. Another—Billy Beyers— was badly wounded and appeared to be dead, but later crawled away. The other four perished. They were Dick Gray, Billy Lang, Charles Snow, and Jim Crane.

Papa and the *rurales* then drove the stolen cattle back to Mexico and returned them to their rightful owners.

The two survivors of the ambush later swore falsely that they had seen Virgil Earp, Wyatt Earp, and Morgan Earp amongst their attackers. No one, save out-of-town members of the Clanton family, really believed them, for the Earp brothers had been seen in Tombstone on the very morning of the ambush.

CHAPTER XVII
WHITE MOUNTAIN UPRISING
1881

What I know of the attack on Fort Apache and of the events precipitating it, I learned from the newspaper. I was not an eyewitness. I mention that battle in this narrative only because it was so significant for the entire Southwest United States, signaling the beginning of a new Apache uprising and evoking nightmares for anyone that had lived through the earlier Apache Wars, which had come to an end only nine years before.

The Chiricahua People were now confined to the San Carlos Reservation. The White Mountain (or Western) Apaches had for years lived peacefully on the Fort Apache Reservation, even supplying the army with scores of scouts.

Throughout the spring and summer of 1881 on the Fort Apache Reservation, the shaman Nock-ay-det-klinne conducted medicine-dance ceremonies, which involved a lot of heavy drinking and use of peyote. Apache scouts often attended these ceremonies and were even known to participate.

Initially, the army was not concerned that these medicine dances posed any type of threat. Local ranchers, however, were convinced that this new activity constituted a prelude to war. Finally, in August, Colonel Eugene Asa Carr, commandant at Ft Apache, agreed to investigate. Toward that end, Carr summoned Nock-ay-det-klinne to report to Fort Apache for an interview. The shaman did not respond.

And so on Monday morning, August 29, Carr led half his command to the village of Cibecue, where Nock-ay-det-klinne was believed to reside. The intention was to arrest him, take him back to the fort, and there to conduct the interview. Colonel Carr only wanted a firm assurance that war was not being planned or even contemplated.

Did Carr overreact? Did he behave foolishly? Perhaps. No doubt, he underestimated the high esteem in which all Apaches held Nock-ay-det-klinne.

In any event, after arresting the shaman and starting the return journey to Fort Apache, Carr and his soldiers were attacked at Cibecue Creek by a large force of Apache warriors. Most of Carr's twenty-three Apache scouts then stripped off their uniforms and joined the attackers. The entire expedition, consisting of five officers and seventy-nine enlisted men of the 6th Cavalry, might well have been wiped out but for a daring rescue staged by a company of White scouts led by Al Sieber and Tom Horn. Only seven soldiers died. Apache losses were much higher. Four of Carr's men were subsequently awarded Congressional Medals of Honor for their parts in this action.

The next day, Carr and his men returned safely to Fort Apache. The medicine man Nock-ay-det-klinne had been mortally wounded during the fighting at Cibecue Creek, and the entire Apache Nation was justly outraged.

On September 1, Fort Apache was fired upon by approximately two hundred White Mountain Apaches. The attack lasted all day, but no attempt was made to breach the walls. Instead, the Apaches cautiously remained at the very edge of rifle range, wounding only a few soldiers, killing none. The soldiers, of course, returned fire, but Apache casualties were undetermined. The White Mountain Uprising continued for about two years.

Many Chiricahua and Warm Springs Apaches, including Geronimo and Chief Naiche (son of Cochise), taking advantage of the fact that the Western Apaches were in revolt, simultaneously broke out from the San Carlos Reservation and fled south to the Sierra Madre Mountains, from there to conduct bloody raids throughout northern Mexico, as well as in Arizona and New Mexico Territories. Naiche would eventually surrender to General George Crook on May 25, 1883. Geronimo would hold out until January of 1884. Nor would this be Geronimo's last breakout.

CHAPTER XVIII
SANDY BOB STAGECOACH ROBBERY
1881

In September of 1881, Miss Nellie—her dry-goods store having proved so very successful—bought half interest in Russ House, the hotel and restaurant established the previous December by Joseph Pascholy. Papa and Miss Nellie were now blissfully in love and shortly to be wed.

About that time, however, Miss Nellie's sister Fanny Cunningham was widowed in another part of the country (I'm not sure exactly where). Miss Nellie sent for Fanny and her five children, who soon arrived in Tombstone to share Miss Nellie's home with her. Initially, Fanny went to work in Miss Nellie's dry-goods store, and the children attended school with me.

A few months later, Fanny would be diagnosed with consumption (also known as the *white plague* or *tuberculosis*), the same disease that had claimed her husband's life. Miss Nellie would then buy a house in Tucson for Fanny and the children and would send them money regularly, so that Fanny could rest and hopefully recover.

By the end of December, the financial burden would become so great that Miss Nellie would have to sell her newly acquired interest in Russ House. Happily, the dry-goods store would continue to thrive.

Papa would still call on Miss Nellie from time to time, but never again would they discuss marriage. Clearly, Miss Nellie's first concern and responsibility would always be for Fanny and the children. The only place for Papa and me in her life would be on the fringes and not at the center.

On the evening of September 8, the Sandy Bob stagecoach traveling from Tombstone to Bisbee was held up by two masked men. There was no strong box onboard, so the bandits shook down the passengers and stole the mail bag.

During the course of the robbery, one of the bandits referred to the money as *sugar*. Former Deputy Sheriff Frank Stilwell, who was known to use that same uncommon term, immediately came under suspicion. An unusual boot print found at the scene of the robbery was identified by a cobbler as being that of a recently repaired boot belonging to Frank Stilwell.

Stilwell's constant companion of late had been Pete Spence, and Pete Spence closely matched the description of the second bandit. Warrants were issued for Stilwell and Spence.

Deputy Sheriffs Billy Breckenridge and Dave Neagle led a posse in pursuit of the two suspects. In that posse were Virgil Earp and Wyatt Earp. Spence and Stilwell were arrested together in Bisbee. They put up no resistance.

At trial, several close associates of Ike Clanton, who had but recently assumed control of his late father's vast criminal empire, testified that the defendants had been playing poker at the Grand Hotel on the night of the robbery. Spence and Stilwell were, therefore, acquitted.

On September 10, even as the occurrences described above were unfolding, two other noteworthy events occurred: one in Tombstone, the other in Galeyville on the far side of the county.

In Tombstone, Marshal Earp attempted to arrest Sherman McMaster, who resisted and escaped. Shots were fired, but no one was hit. That both these men, known to be expert marksmen, missed their targets is remarkable, to say the least.

McMaster, along with Pony Diehl (otherwise known as *Charles Ray*), was wanted in connection with a stagecoach robbery the previous February between Globe City and Florence. Pima County Sheriff Robert Paul had asked Marshal Earp, for reasons known only to himself, not to arrest McMaster until Pony Diehl was in custody. Why the marshal acted so precipitously is something of a mystery.

Nor can I accept that Sherman McMaster ever participated in that holdup, for I had come to know him as a good and honorable man, who was always kind and considerate. He did have some rather unfortunate friends, I admit, but I cannot believe that he would have allowed them to drag him into a situation that might have endangered innocent lives.

In any case, on the same day that Virgil Earp and Sherman McMaster exchanged gunfire, Johnny Ringo and David Estes robbed a poker game in Galeyville. The two cowboys did not even wear masks. They were positively identified by more than a dozen witnesses. At trial, however, none was willing to testify, so both outlaws walked free.

On October 1, Billy Claiborne killed James Hickey in a gunfight at Queen's Saloon in Charleston. Thereafter, Billy demanded that people address him as *Billy the Kid*, the original Billy the Kid no longer being around to object.

On October 13, Virgil Earp, in his capacity as deputy US marshal, rearrested Pete Spence and Frank Stilwell, this time on federal charges of interfering with the US Mail.

The Clantons, the McLaurys, and all their cowboy cronies were incensed that their pals should so unfairly be made to face double jeopardy. *The Tombstone Epitaph* reported "...threats being made that the friends of the accused will 'get the Earps.'"

Wyatt Earp apparently took those threats seriously, for he promptly wired his good friend Doc Holliday, saying that he and his brothers were now anticipating more trouble than they felt that they could handle on their own.

Missing Kate terribly, Doc, you see, had, at last, forgiven her treachery and traveled to Globe City in order to woo her back to him. The couple had kissed and made up, as they always did. Then they had traveled on together to Prescott. When Doc read Wyatt's telegram, he and Kate immediately packed up and returned to Tombstone.

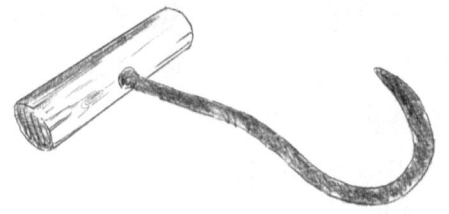

CHAPTER XIX
Lexington Livery Stable
1881

No longer was I a bellhop. An unpleasant incident in late September had soured me on that job. Carrying up the luggage of a newly arrived guest, I had been set upon and very nearly raped. I had, of course, put up a struggle, and I had screamed for help, but I had been unable to get my hand into my pocket to retrieve my little Derringer. Happily, Albert Bilicke and his father had come to my rescue, and in a very timely manner.

I resigned immediately and the very same day found new employment at Lexington Livery Stable, where Papa and I now kept our horses. We had quit doing business with Dexter when we learned that he was withholding the oats we had been paying for, feeding our horses only hay.

Mr Jack Crabtree, the owner of Lexington Livery Stable, promised Papa that he'd look out for me and never allow to occur on his premises any such humiliation as I had so recently endured at the Cosmopolitan Hotel.

Included in my duties were mucking out the stalls, feeding and watering the stock, saddling and unsaddling horses, hitching teams to buggies and wagons, walking lathered animals to cool them down slowly, and grooming horses with a curry comb. I loved the job because I loved horses and I enjoyed being around them, but I could not help resenting my boss's referring to me as his *stable boy*. I asked him once why he did not call me his *stable girl*.

"Thar ain't no such term," he said, "leastwise, not that I ever heared."

I wore dungarees on the job, of course, not as a disguise, but for practical reasons. No one, save a blind man, would have mistaken me for a boy. At almost thirteen years of age, I had a very mature figure and long wavy tresses, of which I was quite proud. Combing my hair each night, I counted a hundred strokes. I do not believe it would be even a slight exaggeration to claim that I was pretty. Certainly, lots of men complimented me on my looks. Happily, none dared to take unwanted liberties with me whilst I worked at Lexington Livery Stable.

"You sure do fill them pants out nicely," one newcomer to Tombstone told me.

Blushing and stammering, I struggled to think of an appropriate response. What the man said was meant as a compliment, I feel sure, but somehow, it made me very uncomfortable.

"See here," said Mr Crabtree, laying his massive hand on the man's shoulder. "That ain't no way to speak to a young lady."

The man immediately apologized. "I do beg your pardon, miss. I meant no disrespect. I was merely expressing my admiration for your appearance."

Doc Holliday, upon his return to Tombstone, said to me, "Why, Miss Falcón, I do declare! I never could have imagined how fetching a lass could be in men's work clothes. You may well set a trend. I predict that by year's end, half the women in Tombstone will have bought themselves Levis."

This prophesy, of course, did not come true. I knew that it would not. People may tolerate nonconformity and eccentricity in reasonably small doses, but they are very slow to embrace new ways themselves.

In the early autumn of 1881, Warren Baxter Earp arrived in Tombstone. Warren was Marshal Earp's youngest brother. A deputy city marshal, he worked as nighttime jailer. The daytime jailer, by the way, was William Soule.

It occurred to me to wonder how many other brothers Marshal Earp had. His older brother James was a bartender in Tombstone and occasionally wore a badge to back Virgil up if called upon. This too seemed to be Wyatt's rôle.

In October of 1881, Wyatt was a full-time gambler and a part-time lawman. Morgan Earp, on the other hand, had quit his Wells Fargo job to become Virgil's chief deputy on a full-time basis. Morgan was a steady hand with an easygoing personality. He reminded me a lot of Fred White, not so much in appearance as in character.

On Tuesday, October 25, Ike Clanton and Tom McLaury arrived in Tombstone to sell a large herd of beef cattle. When their business was done, they began making the rounds of the town's many saloons, drinking heavily and making loud threats against the Earps and Doc Holliday. When news of these threats reached Papa's ears, he made a point to look up the marshal and give him a heads-up.

Virgil Earp dismissed the threats as hollow. "Ike Clanton is a sniveling coward. He's like a dog my Pa once owned. On a chain, that dog seemed vicious. It would bark and snarl at every passing stranger, but turn it loose, and it would crawl whimpering under the house."

"I just thought you ought to know," Papa said. "I shouldn't want them to take you by surprise."

"Thanks, Durango. I appreciate your coming all the way over here to tell me that."

As Papa was turning to leave, Fred Dodge entered the office with a warning even more dire.

"I just received a telegram from JB Ayers in Charleston. It seems that Billy Claiborne, Frank McLaury, and Billy Clanton are planning to meet up with Ike Clanton and Tom McLaury in Tombstone tomorrow afternoon. The five of them mean to have a showdown with you and your brothers."

JB Ayers, a saloonkeeper in Charleston, was Mr Dodge's secret informant, an invaluable source of information about the doings of the cowboys that drank in his establishment.

"Ayers is a good man," Mr Dodge said. "He thinks the threat is real, and I trust his judgment."

"You look terrible, Fred," Marshal Earp observed. "Are you sure you're not ill?"

"I am ill. I've been in bed with a fever for days. But this seemed important enough to drag myself over here. And now, if you'll excuse me, I'm going home and get back into bed, that is if I don't die first along the way."

At the Alhambra Saloon late that night, Ike Clanton and Doc Holliday got into a loud angry quarrel that was broken up by Marshal Earp.

"Cease this immediately," Virgil told the two men, "or by god, I'll arrest you both."

Holliday, very drunk, stumbled off home to bed. Ike then went to the Oriental Saloon in search of Wyatt Earp, with whom he had a brief and very quiet discussion. As the two parted company, Ike was heard to say, "I'll be ready for you in the morning."

Wyatt replied, "There's no money in that, Ike. Go back to Charleston and forget about it."

Ike insisted on having the last word. "Don't think I won't be after you tomorrow morning."

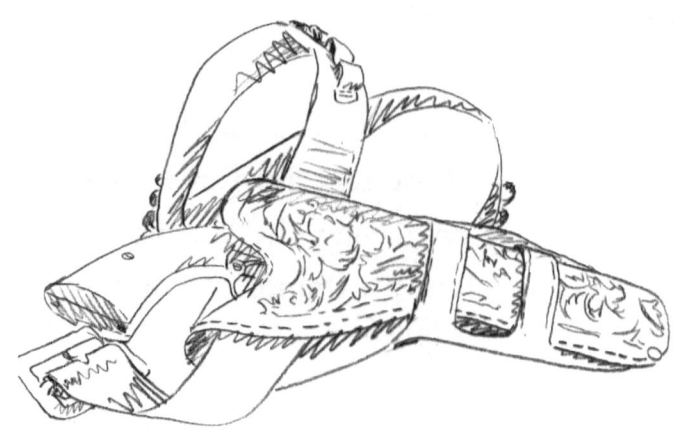

CHAPTER XX
SHOWDOWN ON FREMONT STREET
1881

Sometime after midnight, Papa and Virgil Earp joined a card game in a back room of the Occidental Saloon, which, incidentally, was about half a block west of the Oriental Saloon on Allen Street. Also at the table were Sheriff Behan, Ike Clanton, and Tom McLaury. The game lasted until dawn.

Papa had never been one to stay out all night gambling. He enjoyed a friendly game, to be sure, but usually he would be home in bed well before midnight. On this particular night, however, he was loathe to leave his friend the marshal alone in such dangerous company.

Virgil Earp played cards this night with his revolver in his lap. Papa, in violation of city ordinance, had a storekeeper's gun concealed beneath his coat. That's how concerned he was.

After the game broke up, Ike Clanton collected his rifle and handgun from the West End Corral, where he had checked them the day before upon his arrival in Tombstone. Drifting again from saloon to saloon, he drank heavily and bragged loudly that he intended to kill Doc Holliday today. "And then, God willing, I aim to kill Wyatt Earp and all his kin. I'm just waiting for the cowards to show their faces on the street."

At noon, Ike went to Fly's Boarding House and demanded to see Doc Holliday.

Mollie Fly, alarmed by the fact that Ike was armed, lied. "I'm sorry, Mr Clanton, but Doc didn't come in last night. He's still out."

As soon as Ike had left, Mrs Fly knocked on the door to Doc's room. Kate opened the door a crack and told Mrs Fly that her husband was sleeping off a massive hangover. When Mrs Fly informed Kate that Ike Clanton had been there looking for Doc and that he was armed with a pistol and a rifle, Kate decided to shake Doc awake.

"Curses on that knave!" Doc groaned as he listened to the news. "If God will allow me to live long enough to get my clothes on, Ike will see me a lot sooner than he might wish."

In the early afternoon, Marshal Earp caught up with Ike Clanton, disarmed and arrested him after striking him over the head with the barrel of his pistol. Hauled before Justice of the Peace AO Wallace, Ike was fined twenty-five dollars and released. Marshal Earp then told Ike that, when he was ready to leave town, he could collect his confiscated weapons at the Grand Hotel. Apparently, that information failed to register with Ike, for a few minutes later, he entered Spangenberg's Gun Shop and Hardware Store and attempted to buy a new sidearm. Mr Spangenberg refused to sell him one.

Outside the courtroom, Tom McLaury was waiting for Ike to exit when Wyatt Earp, now wearing a deputy's badge, approached him.

"Are you heeled? Or are you not?" Wyatt demanded to know.

"I am not," McLaury lied, for as he turned, his coat opened enough to reveal a six-gun in his holster.

In the blink of an eye, Wyatt whipped his own gun out and buffaloed McLaury, exactly as his brother Virgil had earlier done Ike Clanton. Wyatt was about to disarm the unconscious man and arrest him, when Allen English arose from a nearby bench and interceded.

Allen English, you should know, was a modestly successful lawyer in Tombstone. Papa and I had known him casually for almost two years, and never once had I seen him completely sober. On the other hand, I had never seen him falling-down drunk either. He had plenty of clients, and his win-lose ratio was very nearly as good as that of other lawyers in Tombstone.

"Allow me, please, Mr Earp, to give you some free legal advice. I don't make a habit of doing that."

"What's on your mind, Mr English?" Wyatt asked.

"I must remind you that you are only a *special* deputy and not on the city payroll. You are authorized, when wearing that badge, to act in support of the marshal or his regular deputies, but you do not have the authority to initiate arrests on your own. For the action you have just taken, you could be subject to prosecution for assault and battery. Drop this matter at once. Your brothers are going to need you to back them up before this day is out."

Wyatt nodded his acquiescence and allowed Tom McLaury's limp form to slump back onto the floor. He did not even disarm the man, but stalked off to buy himself a cigar and to smoke it in solitude.

The day was breezy and quite chilly, but not what I'd call bitterly cold. A light blanket of snow lay on the ground. The sun shone brightly. The snow would soon melt away.

I spent that morning in class, but my mind was elsewhere. I skipped the afternoon session. Nor was I the only one to do so. When Burt Alford saw me slip out of the schoolyard during our lunch break, he followed me.

Please understand, I did not make a habit of playing hooky, but I could not bear to miss whatever was going to happen today. Everyone knew that a gunfight was likely to occur. I was hopeful that the outcome would prove to be the beginning of the end for the cowboys. Anyway, I had already learned just about everything that this dinky little school had to teach me. I had lost all interest in repeating the same lessons I had been doing for years.

Burt Alford was two or three years my senior and could not understand why I refused to accept him as my beau. Today, I did allow him to tag along beside me. Putting up with him was easier than figuring out a way to lose him. And so it was that Burt and I both witnessed the big showdown.

At around 2:30 in the afternoon, nineteen-year-old Billy Clanton, Frank McLaury, and Billy

Claiborne arrived in Tombstone. They went directly to the Grand Hotel Saloon, but seeing Doc Holliday there, they decided to drink elsewhere.

Twenty minutes later, they had slaked their thirst, met up with Ike Clanton and Tom McLaury, and been joined by fellow cowboy Wes Fuller. The six men were gathered at the OK Corral, shouting threats against the Earps to every passerby.

Apparently, however, they had a change of plans. Exiting the OK Corral by a back entrance, they proceeded westward on Fremont Street. All six were afoot, leading their mounts.

Between Fly's Boarding House and the Harwoods' home next door, there was a narrow yard through which one must pass to reach CS Fly's Photographic Studio directly behind the boarding house. It was in this very yard that Papa and I had stood chatting with Mollie Fly as we had waited for her husband to finish taking Doc Holliday's portrait. Today, this yard was where the six cowboys stopped to await the Earps.

Sheriff Behan arrived first and nervously begged the cowboys to hand over their weapons. They refused, and he went away.

Virgil Earp, meanwhile, went to the Wells Fargo office to borrow a shotgun, which he then concealed beneath his overcoat. Mayor Clum offered the assistance of the Vigilance Committee to help disarm the cowboys, but Marshal Earp said *no, thank you. This was a job for professionals.* Deputy City Marshals Andy Bronk and Warren Earp also offered to help but were instructed to keep to their regular duties. Virgil Earp, Morgan Earp, Wyatt Earp, and Doc Holliday alone would handle the situation. All four had badges pinned conspicuously to their heavy overcoats.

"I'm so damned hung over," Holliday complained as the four men set out to confront the outlaws, "that I'm not sure I could hit a man at ten paces."

"Here," Virgil suggested, "you take the shotgun. Give me your cane."

None of the lawmen had gun belts on. Wyatt had his pistol in hand as they turned onto Fremont Street. The other three had pistols stuck in the waistbands of their trousers. Virgil's gun hand rested on the butt of his. In his other hand, he carried Doc Holliday's walking stick.

Sheriff Behan met them in front of Bauer's Butcher Shop and begged them not to proceed. "I've disarmed them already. You don't need to go any farther."

"I am greatly relieved that they are disarmed," said Virgil, shifting the cane from his left hand to his right. "But I believe I'll walk on up there and have a word with them all the same."

Wyatt, hearing that the cowboys had been disarmed, put his six-shooter in his overcoat pocket. Clearly, he no longer expected to have to use it.

Sheriff Behan shouted after them, "If you go up there, they'll murder you all."

Burt and I had been trailing along at a distance of about half a block behind the Earps and Doc Holliday. When they paused to exchange words with Sheriff Behan, we, of course, hung back. Then the sheriff turned to join the parade, and Burt and I brought up the rear.

As the lawmen approached the cowboys, Wes Fuller spread his coat wide to show that there was no gun in his holster. He then climbed into the saddle and trotted off down the street.

Simultaneously, Sheriff Behan stepped through the front door of Fly's Boarding House. I clearly heard Mr Buck Fly demand to know why he wasn't out there backing up the marshal. I could not understand the sheriff's muttered response.

"Throw up your hands," I heard Marshal Earp shout. "I want your guns."

Burt and I were in a terrible position, directly behind the lawmen. When the shooting started, any bullets missing them might very well find us. I remember thinking how cross Papa would be if I got myself shot. Burt and I bolted at the same instant, he in one direction, I in another.

"Hold it!" I heard Marshal Earp cry out. "I don't want that."

I turned to look over my shoulder and saw that Frank McLaury and Billy Clanton had both drawn and cocked their pistols and were aiming them at the lawmen.

Billy Clanton fired the first shot at Virgil Earp. Virgil drew his weapon and fired a split second later, hitting Frank McLaury in the abdomen. Frank went down momentarily, but quickly got back up. Billy Claiborne and Ike Clanton immediately turned and ran from the scene. None of the lawmen fired at the two fleeing men.

Tom McLaury, hiding behind his mount, began firing across his saddle. The horse, of course, would not stand still, and so Tom's aim was off. I do not believe he ever hit anyone. Doc Holliday stepped around the back end of Tom McLaury's horse and fired both barrels of the shotgun at the cowboy, who dropped his pistol and staggered off westward down Fremont Street to fall dead at the corner of Third Street.

Tossing the empty shotgun aside, Doc drew his pistol and began firing at Frank McLaury.

Gunsmoke now filled the air so thickly that opponents standing only six to ten feet apart could scarcely see one another. Morgan, having been hit, fired from the ground, wounding Billy Clanton in the wrist.

Shifting his gun from right hand to left, Billy continued to fire until Wyatt dropped him.

Frank McLaury, badly wounded, ran past the lawmen into Fremont Street to where his horse had shied. Firing his last bullet, he managed to hit Doc

Holliday, who was only slightly wounded because the bullet was deflected by a pocket gun.

Even so, Doc was furious. "That son-of-a-bitch has shot me. I'll kill him." And so saying, he shot Frank McLaury in the head just as Frank was retrieving his rifle from his saddle scabbard.

Wyatt and Doc now turned their attention to helping Virgil and Morgan, both of whom lay on the ground wounded. Neither Wyatt nor Doc noticed that Billy Clanton, lying on the ground mortally wounded, was struggling to raise his pistol. Buck Fly, bearing a Henry rifle, came running from the boarding house to kick the gun from the dying outlaw's hand.

The gunfight had lasted less than a minute, but that fraction of a minute had felt to me like hours. In the midst of any deadly struggle, time seems to slow to a crawl. I wonder why that is.

Virgil and Morgan were treated by Dr Goodfellow. Doc's graze did not require immediate attention. Wyatt had come through without so much as a scratch.

Not long after this shootout, which, curiously, came to be known as the *Gunfight at the OK Corral*,

Territorial Governor Frederick Tritle authorized the formation of a company of Arizona Rangers to help enforce the law in the territory.

CHAPTER XXI
THE BAR DOUBLE D RANCH
1881

On the very evening after the big gunfight, Mr Frank Patterson (not the outlaw cowboy of the same name) called on us at the Cosmopolitan Hotel to offer Papa a deal on a little ranch that had been used by the McLaurys.

"It's not very sizable, Durango," he admitted. "It's rocky as hell, and grass is sparse, but it does have water. It's definitely not cattle country, but you could raise goats there, I suppose, or maybe horses. Mustangs love that country. I'll lease it to you for next to nothing, or I'll sell it cheap, whichever you prefer."

"Gaby and I'll ride out to Soldier's Hole tomorrow and look it over," Papa said. "I'll get back to you in a day or two. And thanks for thinking of me first, Mr Patterson."

"Tombstone isn't exactly rife with honest men, Durango. You have an admirable reputation. That's why I came to you. I don't want that property ever again to be used as a refuge for outlaws. I'd have sent the McLaurys packing ages ago, except for the fact that I was so frightened of Frank. He was a mean son-of-a-bitch. I'm glad he's dead."

I fell in love with the ranch at first sight. The main cabin and outbuildings were nothing to speak of—they were wretched, in fact—but the surrounding countryside was just about the most beautiful I had ever seen. I knew immediately that I wanted to live there forever. I hoped that we could buy that little piece of land and not just lease it.

"Can we afford it, Papa?" I asked. "I have almost sixty dollars saved. You can add that to whatever you have in the bank."

Papa smiled tolerantly. "I think I can swing this deal without your contribution, Gaby."

"But, Papa," I insisted. "I want this to be my ranch too. Let me help pay for it, so we can be partners for real. Okay?"

Papa offered me his hand to shake. "Alright, partner. Let's go look up Mr Patterson and see how much he wants for this place."

A deal was soon struck, and Papa and I became the new owners of what had been the McLaurys' original ranch. We renamed it the *Bar Double D*.

Before actually moving out to the ranch, Papa and I made sure that no trace of the McLaurys remained. We loaded all their bedding, lanterns, kitchen utensils, tools, tack, guns, ammunition, and clothes into a battered old buckboard we found in the barn. There was no stock whatever on the ranch. No doubt, some of the McLaurys' former associates had already been there. Then, whilst I performed a thorough cleaning of the main cabin, Papa hitched our newly bought team to the buckboard and drove it into town to turn the wagon and those meager possessions over to the brother of the deceased.

The McLaurys, you see, had an elder sibling, who happened to be a judge in Texas. Will McLaury came all the way to Tombstone to help Phineas Clanton build a murder case against the Earps and Doc Holliday.

Judge Spicer held a preliminary hearing to determine whether or not there was sufficient evidence for the case to proceed to trial. That hearing lasted more than a month and fully exonerated the Earps and Doc Holliday, though not before any number of witnesses, the sheriff included, perjured themselves. Thank goodness, the testimony of so many other witnesses supported the defendants' version of events, as, of course, did every scrap of physical evidence.

Entirely on my own, I designed a brand for our little ranch, which Papa approved and successfully registered. It featured a small d (for *Little Durango*) backed up against an uppercase D (for *Big Durango*), and there was a bar across the top. A Tombstone blacksmith wrought us a branding iron. Our business plan was to capture and break wild horses to sell.

We also acquired more than a dozen hens and a rooster. There was already an enclosure with a hen house, although in bad repair. Together, Papa and I made it like new. Feeding the chickens and gathering eggs became one of my daily chores. I learned, too, how to wring the necks of chickens and pluck their feathers, but I never got past being distressed by the necessary cruelty of it. Even so, my enjoyment of eating chicken was in no way diminished.

I dropped out of school, of course, but Papa insisted that we read books together, in order that my education continue. Every evening by lantern light, he would read a chapter aloud to me. Then I should read the next to him. In that way, we read our way through *The Decline and Fall of the Roman Empire*, Caesar's *Gallic Wars*, *The Iliad* and *The Odyssey*, *The Dialogues of Plato*, and any number of other works.

We read poetry too, both English and Spanish, for Papa was a great lover of poetry, and little by little, I came to appreciate it too, though never have I managed to derive as much pleasure from it as Papa clearly does.

I wore ranch clothes exclusively (cotton pants, high-top boots, leather leggings or chaps, a wide-brimmed straw sombrero, and sturdy gauntlets). I had outgrown all my dresses, and we had not the wherewithal to replace them. Nor was I ever without my gun belt. Of course, being a law-abiding citizen, I checked my Colt with Mr Crabtree whenever we ventured into Tombstone. The Derringer was with me at all times but well concealed.

I was a crack shot now, for Papa and I practiced together on a daily basis, and anyway, gun handling seemed to come naturally to me.

As every year, Papa and I traveled to Los Neri for Christmas. We did our level best to persuade Horace to come live with us at the Bar Double D, but he would not even consider it.

"I can't understand why you and Papa don't just live here," he said.

I couldn't explain it then, but Los Neri was simply too small a world for us. Papa and I shared an adventurous spirit that was missing in Horace and an unquenchable curiosity to experience first hand as much of the world as humanly possible. Horace too was curious about the world, but he was content to learn exclusively through reading.

On Christmas Eve, the Bird Cage Theater opened on Allen Street in Tombstone. What Schieffelin Hall was for Tombstone's gentry, the Bird Cage was for miners, stockmen, and anyone not exactly genteel. Only a few months after the Bird Cage's grand opening, the *New York Times* would describe this entertainment palace, which, by the way, included a bar and a bordello, as "the wildest, wickedest night spot between Basin Street and the Barbary Coast."

Four nights after the Bird Cage Theater opened, Marshal Virgil Earp, now recovered from the wound he received in the Fremont Street shootout, was ambushed in the street as he made his nightly rounds. Gravely wounded, he was carried to Dr Goodfellow's office. He was not expected to recover.

The next morning, Wyatt Earp sent the following telegraph to US Marshal Crawley Dake in Prescott:

Virgil Earp was shot by concealed assassins last night. His wounds are fatal. Telegraph me appointment with power to appoint deputies. Local authorities are doing nothing. The lives of other citizens are threatened.

Wyatt Earp

CHAPTER XXII
DAHTESTE AND GOUYEN
1882

Thanks to the expertise of Dr Goodfellow, Virgil Earp did not, in fact, die from his wounds, but his shattered arm would never again be useful to him. Virgil would eventually return to law enforcement. At present, however, he was unable to perform his duties.

Virgil's temporary replacement as city marshal of Tombstone was James Flynn. In a special election, however, Flynn would soon be replaced by Deputy Sheriff Dave Neagle, who has since become one of the most-celebrated lawmen in the West.

Shortly after the first of the year, a posse consisting of Wyatt Earp, Morgan Earp, Fred Dodge, and Deputy Sheriff Charlie Smith stopped at the Bar Double D to refill canteens and to trade for fresh mounts. They were in pursuit of stagecoach robbers, they told us. Five minutes after their arrival, they were gone again. I never heard whether they caught up with the bandits or not.

In Tombstone on January 17, James Flynn arrested Johnny Ringo and Doc Holliday, who were quarreling loudly in public. The angry disagreement was escalating rapidly when Flynn intervened to prevent a gunfight in the street. The two men appeared before Judge Spicer and each paid a fine. Doc Holliday was released, but Johnny Ringo was immediately re-arrested for a train robbery in Galeyville. After spending the weekend in jail, Ringo posted bail and was released as well.

It was about this time that Lou Rickabaugh sold his interest in the gambling concession at the Oriental Saloon back to Milt Joyce, an ally of the Clantons and a member of the Ten Percent Ring. Wyatt Earp, refusing to be in partnership with Mr Joyce, then sold his interest as well.

On January 30, arrest warrants were issued for Pony Diehl, Ike Clanton, and Phineas Clanton for the attempted murder of Virgil Earp. Ike and Phineas were taken into custody to stand trial, but Pony Diehl managed somehow to evade capture.

Johnny Barnes, Johnny Ringo, Hank Swilling and Pete Spence were also implicated in the assassination plot but evidence sufficient to justify arrest warrants could never be uncovered.

Papa received a summons for jury duty and left me alone at the ranch for a few days. We had thirty horses to be saddle-trained for the army and only a few more days to complete the contract. We badly needed the money. One of us simply had to keep working.

At trial, Sherman McMaster testified that, in Charleston shortly after the shooting, he had casually asked Ike Clanton what he knew of the attempt on

Virgil's life and that Clanton had replied, "I'll have to go back and do the job over."

Ike Clanton's hat had even been found at the site of the shooting, but insomuch as several of the Clantons' cowboy cronies provided the accused men with alibis, convictions were impossible.

In any event, it was whilst Papa was away that I was paid a visit by my childhood friend Dahteste and another young Apache woman called *Gouyen.* Both were bleeding from bullet wounds. I patched them up as well as I knew how. I fed them and put them to bed to rest. I wanted to ride into Tombstone and fetch Dr Goodfellow, but they would not hear of it.

It surprised me considerably that Dahteste had known where to find me.

"Apaches watch and know all that goes on in the world of the Whites, but the Whites know little of the Apaches," Dahteste said by way of explanation.

I hated to think what mischief these two had been about to get them both shot. I feared that they had joined the uprising, but they did not speak of it, and I did not ask. Well armed and dressed for battle, they arrived afoot. When, after two days' rest, they were well enough to travel, I gave them provisions for the trail and two horses, then I bid them safe journey to wherever they were headed.

CHAPTER XXIII
MURDER MOST FOUL
1882

When the Clantons were acquitted of conspiracy and attempted murder, Wyatt Earp was so discouraged that he tendered his resignation as deputy US marshal. Crawley Dake begged him to reconsider and to stay on the job. Reluctantly, Wyatt agreed, and Marshal Dake tore up Wyatt's letter of resignation.

To pay for extra deputies (five dollars a day), Wyatt mortgaged his home to lawyer James G Howard for three hundred sixty-five dollars. Howard would eventually have to foreclose.

On a Saturday night, March 18, Morgan Earp was murdered as he played billiards with Dan Tipton at Campbell and Hatch's Saloon and Billiard Parlor just four doors up from the Cosmopolitan Hotel on Allen Street. The shooter stood in the dark alley behind the building and fired through a glass window in the back door. The fatal bullet passed through Morgan's body and wounded another man, George Berry. Mr Berry and Wyatt Earp had been chatting together as they watched the game. Also present was the proprietor, Bob Hatch.

The next morning, Wyatt organized a bodyguard to protect Virgil, who was not yet recovered from the attempt on his life the previous December. Deputized were James Earp and Warren Earp, Doc Holliday, Sherman McMaster, Turkey Creek Jack Johnson, Harelip Charlie Smith, Dan Tipton, and Texas Jack Vermillion.

On Monday morning, two days after the shooting, Wyatt and his deputies set out for

Contention City, where they meant to put Morgan's casket on a train bound for Colton, California, the Earps' family home. Morgan's wife Louisa, by the way, was already in Colton visiting her parents-in-law. Morgan was to be buried in Colton, and James was to accompany his casket in a box car.

The plan was then to drive Virgil and his wife Allie to Benson, there to put them on a passenger train also bound for California. James's wife Bessie and Wyatt's wife by common law Mattie Blaylock remained in Tombstone. They too would leave for California a few days later, as would Josephine (or Sadie) Marcus, the former Mrs Behan, who happened also to be the future Mrs Wyatt Earp.

Incidentally, I have heard it suggested in recent years that Wyatt and Josephine might have had an affair in Tombstone, but if so, they certainly were discreet, for I never saw any evidence of intimacy between them. Nor did I, at the time, get even a whiff of gossip to that effect. Indeed, it would have been totally out of character for Wyatt to disrespect Mattie by carrying on behind her back.

In any event, Papa and I first learned of Morgan's murder on Monday morning when we drove a score of horses into Tombstone for delivery to various stables that had placed orders with us.

"Cut out seven," Papa told me as we entered the town. "Deliver three to Dunbar's and four to Crabtree's. I'll deal with the rest. We can meet up at the Cosmopolitan for a late breakfast or an early lunch, whichever you prefer."

"Why don't I take those for Mr Williams as well?" I offered. "The Wells Fargo Corral is directly across the street from Dunbar's."

"Sure," Papa agreed. "That makes sense. I'll see you in an hour or so."

By the time all our horses had been delivered and we had been paid, we had heard all the gory details of Morgan's murder, and I had even managed to pick up intelligence that Ike Clanton, Frank Stilwell, and Hank Swilling were planning tonight to ambush Virgil in Tucson, where he and Allie would have to change trains.

"I'd better skip breakfast," Papa said when I told him what I had overheard. "I'm going to ride to Contention City and warn Wyatt. You go ahead and eat. I'll see you back at the ranch tonight."

We had just sat down in the restaurant at the Cosmopolitan. I was famished. All I had had since supper the night before was a cup of coffee. After Papa left, however, it occurred to me that, if he missed the Earps at Contention City, he would likely be unable to catch up with them in Benson before Virgil's train left. I decided, therefore, to skip breakfast myself and ride directly to Benson.

As I was mounting to leave, I was hailed by Fred Dodge, to whom I then gave the same information that I had given to Papa. I explained to him what I meant to do and why. "If you happen to see Papa before I do, please let him know where I am. I don't want him to worry, but I feel that I must do this."

"Yes, of course, Gaby," said Mr Dodge. "I'm glad you told me. I think I'll wire the deputy US marshal in Tucson. Maybe he can take steps to prevent this ambush from occurring."

I found the Earp party at the Benson Railroad Station. Allie Earp in a black dress, I noticed, was wearing her husband's gunbelt. In the tightest notch, that gunbelt was too big for her waist, but it fit nicely around her hips. Virgil himself had a brand new Smith and Wesson break-top revolver similar to Papa's stuck in his waistband, where he could easily reach it with his good hand. I warned them that Ike and some of his cowboys were already in Tucson intending to make another attempt on Virgil's life.

"Thanks, Gaby," said Wyatt. "I ought to have anticipated such a move from Ike."

Wyatt then went to the counter and bought tickets for himself and for his brother Warren, Doc Holliday, Turkey Creek Jack Johnson, and Sherman McMaster. The other members of his posse he dismissed and sent back to Tombstone. When the train arrived, the reduced posse boarded with Virgil and Allie.

I returned to the ranch to find Papa there waiting for me. Happily, he was not upset with me for having gone to Benson. In fact, he said he was proud of me for thinking of it in the first place and then taking action.

A coroner's jury, meanwhile, was conducting an inquest into the death of Morgan Earp. Based on testimony by Marietta Duarte (wife of Pete Spence) and other witnesses, that jury made the following determination:

> Morgan Earp...came to his death in the city of Tombstone on the 18th day of March, 1882...by reason of a gunshot or pistol wound inflicted at the hands of Pete Spence, Frank Stilwell, a party by the name of Freis, and two Indian half-breeds, one whose name is *Charlie*. The name of the other is not ascertained.

The man whose name the court recorder spelled *F-R-E-I-S* was Frederick Bode, otherwise known as *Freeze*. *Freis* was just a misspelling of *Freeze*. The half-breed known as *Charlie*, was, of course, Florentino Cruz, who may or may not have been Florentino Saiz. The other unidentified half-breed, it would later be learned, was Hank Swilling.

Pete Spence, fearing the wrath of Wyatt Earp, turned himself in to his pal Sheriff Behan, who would, of course, release him when imminent danger had passed.

In Tucson, the Earp party was met by Deputy US Marshal Joseph W Evans. Virgil and Allie dined at the Porter Hotel as Wyatt and his deputies stood watch nearby. The short walk back to the train station, however, exhausted Virgil to the extent that he had to be carried up the steps of the Pullman car.

As the train prepared to leave the station, Wyatt spotted Frank Stilwell and another man with shotguns near the tracks. Gunfire erupted. Stilwell died instantly. The other man, unidentified, managed to slip away in the darkness. Witnesses had earlier that night seen Stilwell in the company of Ike Clanton and Hank Swilling.

To *The Denver Republican*, Wyatt would later make the following statement regarding the shooting in Tucson:

> I ran straight for Stilwell. It was he who killed my brother. What a coward he was! He couldn't shoot when I came near him. He stood there helpless and trembling for his life. As I rushed upon him, he put out his hands and clutched at my shotgun. I let go both barrels, and he tumbled down dead and mangled at my feet.

Tucson Justice of the Peace Charles Meyer issued arrest warrants for Wyatt Earp and his deputies. Pima County Sheriff Robert Paul was a close friend and an ally of the Earps. I hate to think what an awkward position those warrants put him in.

With Virgil and Allie safely on their way to California, Wyatt and his deputies left Tucson afoot in the middle of the night. They walked nine miles to the Papago Freight Stop and there flagged down the mid-night train. By the following day, they were back in Tombstone, preparing to go after the other suspects in Morgan's murder. They could not have known that Pete Spence was already in jail.

Sheriff Paul wired Sheriff Behan to arrest and hold Wyatt and the others named in the warrants he held. The telegraph operator in Tombstone, before delivering that message to Behan, warned Wyatt of its contents and agreed to sit on it for a few hours whilst Wyatt organized a federal posse to go after others implicated in Morgan's murder.

That posse consisted of Wyatt's brother Warren, Doc Holliday, Turkey Creek Jack Johnson, Sherman McMaster, Fred Dodge, Texas Jack Vermillion, Dan Tipton (a Civil War veteran of the Union Navy), Harelip Charlie Smith, Louis Cooley (a stagecoach driver for Wells Fargo), and Johnny Green.

They rode first to Charleston, then to the Clanton ranch. At neither of these locations did they find any of their suspects. On Wednesday, March 22, Wyatt divided his posse into two groups in order to cover more territory. The group he led, including Warren Earp, Doc Holliday, Sherman McMaster, and Turkey Creek Jack Johnson, went to Pete Spence's ranch in hopes of finding Spence there.

Caretaker Theodore Judah informed the lawmen that his boss was currently in jail in Tombstone but that Indian Charlie was somewhere on the property cutting wood. The posse rode on in the direction indicated by Judah. A few hundred yards up the trail, they encountered their prey. A brief gun battle ensued, and Indian Charlie was slain. That evening, the two contingents of the posse reunited.

The next morning, Wyatt sent Smith and Tipton back into Tombstone to see what information they could gather. Obviously, the men they sought were in hiding.

"We need more funds, too," Wyatt told them. "Try to raise at least a thousand dollars. Then meet us at Iron Springs, and don't lose any time. We'll be waiting there."

Wyatt then directed Fred Dodge and Louis Cooley to request financial support from their employer Wells Fargo. Johnny Green was sent on a scouting mission. Wyatt and the rest then hurried to Iron Springs to await the arrival of Tipton and Smith and the others. There, quite unexpectedly, they blundered into the campsite of nine outlaw cowboys: Curly Bill Brocius, Pony Diehl, Johnny Barnes, Frank Patterson, Milt Hicks and Bill Hicks, Ed Lyle and Johnny Lyle, and Bill Johnson.

A gunfight immediately broke out. Wyatt killed Curly Bill Brocius with a shotgun belonging to Fred Dodge. Then with his pistol, he fatally wounded Johnny Barnes. Milt Hicks was also hit, but by whom it was unclear. In any event, Hicks later recovered. The other outlaws escaped unharmed.

During the shooting, Turkey Creek Jack Johnson had his mount shot out from under him. Doc Holliday heroically pulled him from beneath the fallen horse and helped him to safety even as bullets were flying all about them. Wyatt's clothes were shot full of holes and the horn of his saddle was shot away, but his actual person was untouched. Miraculously, none of the posse members suffered wounds that day.

Meanwhile in Tombstone, Dan Tipton and Charlie Smith were arrested by Sheriff Behan and held overnight. The next day, however, Judge AJ Felter ordered their release. Tipton and Smith solicited funds from business owners and mine owners, most of whom demanded that their contributions be kept secret.

Not so Mr Martin R Peel of the Tombstone Milling and Mining Company. He was proud to have it known that he supported the Earps, who, after all, stood for law and order. On Saturday night, March 25, in front of several witnesses, he was murdered by two masked men.

The victim's father, Judge Bryant L Peel, then published an open letter in *The Tombstone Epitaph*:

Perhaps I am not in a condition to express a clear, deliberate opinion, but I would say to the good citizens of Cochise County there are three things you have to do. There is a class of cut-throats among you, and you can never convict them in court. You must combine and protect yourselves and wipe them out, or you must give up the country to them. Else you will be murdered one at a time, as my son has been.

Sheriff Behan had, by this time, organized a large posse of his own and was currently in pursuit of Wyatt Earp's federal posse. That county posse included Johnny Ringo, Phineas Clanton, and other known outlaws.

At Fort Grant, Sheriff Behan and Undersheriff Woods attempted to enlist the aid of army scouts in tracking the federal posse, even offering a five hundred dollar reward. The scouts refused to help.

Vastly outnumbered, the Earp posse was finally forced to flee for New Mexico Territory. Wyatt and his men stopped at the Percy Ranch to refill canteens and to exchange their mounts for fresh ones, but the Percys were so terrified of the

Clanton cowboys that they withheld their usual warm hospitality.

Papa and I, on the other hand, refused to be intimidated by anyone. Wyatt and those of his men that were still with him supped with us, then passed the night in our barn before setting out the next morning for Henry Hooker's Sierra Bonita Ranch. Behan's posse was close behind them when they arrived there. Mr Hooker offered to help them make a stand, but Wyatt elected, instead, to ride into the hills and wait until Behan's posse had moved on.

The next day, Wyatt and the other wanted men in his posse plus Harelip Charlie Smith and Texas Jack Vermillion rode out of Arizona Territory to meet up with Bat Masterson in Albuquerque. Smith returned a few months later and even managed to step back into his former position as deputy sheriff.

Fred Dodge, Johnny Green, and Louis Cooley, of course, never left the territory. Cooley was arrested for aiding and abetting the Earps, but Judge Spicer dismissed the charges as frivolous.

In the next election, Jerome L Ward was to replace Johnny Behan as sheriff. Ward would then serve only two years before being defeated by Bob Hatch, half owner of the billiard parlor and saloon where Morgan Earp was slain.

CHAPTER XXIV
MARIETTA AND MODESTA
1882

Having given testimony against her husband and his co-conspirators, Marietta Duarte and her mother Modesta Cortéz sought refuge at the Bar Double D. It was widely known that Pete Spence had sworn to kill them both, and he would likely be out of jail soon.

The two women arrived at the ranch afoot an hour or so after dark and hailed us from a distance. Papa went out to meet them and invite them in. Trail-worn, dirty, and totally exhausted from their long walk, they were each carrying a carpetbag, which they dropped just inside the door. I offered them water and seats at the table.

"We hate to impose on you, Durango," said Marietta when she had satisfied her thirst, "but we need a safe place to hide out for a while."

I was at the stove making coffee and preparing them something to eat.

"Let us work for you," Modesta begged. "We'll cook and clean house and do whatever else needs doing. Please, don't say *no*, Durango. We have nowhere else to go and no one else to turn to."

"Do you really imagine that I should ever refuse anyone sanctuary?" Papa asked. "You're more than welcome to stay here. You must understand, though, that I cannot afford to pay you a regular salary. We barely get by from month to month ourselves, but whenever we sell some horses, I'll give you part of the proceeds, whatever I can spare. No one should have to work for free."

"That is more than generous," Modesta said. "Thank you, Durango. You are a true *caballero.*"

"Maybe you find me desirable," Marietta suggested shyly. "I could be your woman if you want me."

"No one could fail to find you desirable, Marietta," said Papa gallantly, "but I am not the kind of man to take unfair advantage of someone's unfortunate situation."

"Oh, but it wouldn't be like that," Marietta protested. "I'd be pleased to be your woman. I ought to have said that in the first place." Clearly, she was embarrassed to be speaking thus. "If I am being inappropriate, please forgive me. I am just an ignorant *campesina* with no social graces, but I could be fiercely loyal to a man that does not beat me and my mother, as Pete used to do."

Papa glanced anxiously at Marietta's mother, whose expression gave away nothing, and then at me. So amused was I that I had to struggle to contain my mirth.

"Marietta," Papa said at last, "perhaps you and I could discuss in private the nature of our future relationship."

"Of course, Durango. Whatever you say."

Papa and I had been on friendly terms with Marietta and Modesta since shortly after our arrival in Tombstone. We had often commiserated with them for the abuse heaped on them by Pete Spence, but I had never once imagined their becoming part of our household. Life can be so unpredictable. Mind you, I was not in the least unhappy with this turn of events. I had long felt that Papa needed a wife. And now it looked as though he was to have one, if only by common law. I just hoped that Miss Nellie would not feel betrayed.

Our main ranch house was but a shabby little one-room cabin with one bed and one cot. On the night of their arrival, Modesta and Marietta slept in the barn, which happened, by the way, to be the sturdiest structure on the ranch. By the following night, however, Papa and Marietta had agreed together to become a couple. Thenceforth, they would share the bed in the house, and Modesta and I should sleep in the barn. I dragged my cot out to the tack room, and Modesta laid a bedroll in the loose hay in the loft above.

Sometime after midnight, the Bar Double D was attacked by night riders. Five cowboys galloped into the yard and began pouring pistol and rifle fire into the house. I immediately reached for my Colt. Still in my night clothes, I ran to the door of the barn, and shot two of the raiders out of their saddles before the other three wheeled their horses and fled into the night. I recognized them all, for the moon was bright and none was masked.

Marietta in a flannel night gown flew from the house. "Come quick, please. Durango's been hit. He's bleeding badly."

By now, Modesta had climbed down from the loft and followed us into the house. It was she that took charge of treating Papa's wounds. I fetched her a bottle of whiskey to disinfect the wounds and an armful of rags to serve as bandages. Marietta put water on to boil. Following the example of Dr Goodfellow, we washed our own hands thoroughly and sterilized the knife and the needle we expected to use.

When the bullets had been removed—three of different calibers—and the wounds sewed shut, Papa rested. The eastern sky was just beginning to brighten. I put coffee on, and Marietta began preparing breakfast.

"I'm afraid that we brought this on you, Gaby," Modesta apologized. "I'm so very sorry."

"This was not about you," I told her. "Nobody even knows that you are here. This is because Papa and I helped the Earps."

"Are you sure?"

"Oh, yes. We've been expecting trouble. But somehow, we thought we'd see it coming and be able to deal with it."

One of the two men that I had slain the night before was Frederick Bode (also called *Freeze*). The other was known to me as a Clanton cowboy, but not by name. The three that got away were Johnny Ringo, Pony Diehl, and half-breed Hank Swilling. I resolved to kill all three at the very first opportunity.

After breakfast, I set about to bury the slain outlaws, but the ground was so rocky that I soon gave up and dragged the bodies far from the house and rolled them into a ravine. As far as I know, they have never been discovered there. Nor have I ever revisited the site.

CHAPTER XXV
GOATS AND MUSTANGS
1882

Papa's wounds healed quickly, but he was only able to get about with a crutch. One of the bullets, you see, had struck his hip. Riding was almost unbearably painful for him. Happily, we still owned a wagon and a team.

198

We were holding about fifty mustangs, most of them yet unbroken, in corrals on the ranch. The task of turning them into saddle mounts now fell entirely to me. It was a job I hated because it was so hard on my body. Mind you, it was a job I did well. The horse has not been born that can unseat me. But I always felt, after a rough ride, as if all my insides had been rearranged. My muscles ached too, and I had bruises in places I cannot mention.

When, at last, the task was done and all the mustangs had been delivered, Papa suggested that, in future, we might offer horses for sale unbroken. "We'd have to take a lot less, of course, but we'll save on hay if the turnover is fast enough."

Until now, our customer base had consisted almost entirely of livery stables, city folk, and the army. Henceforth, we would be selling primarily to cattlemen capable of breaking the horses themselves.

Working together to capture more wild horses, Modesta and I became quite good friends. It was she, in fact, that first suggested that we could supplement our income by raising goats, the care of which she herself would assume, for she had been brought up on a goat farm in Sonora and claimed to know everything there was to know about raising goats.

Tombstone butcher shops, it turned out, were eager to buy our goats, *cabrito* being a favorite meat in the Borderlands. And what luxury it was always to have cheese and fresh milk for our own table!

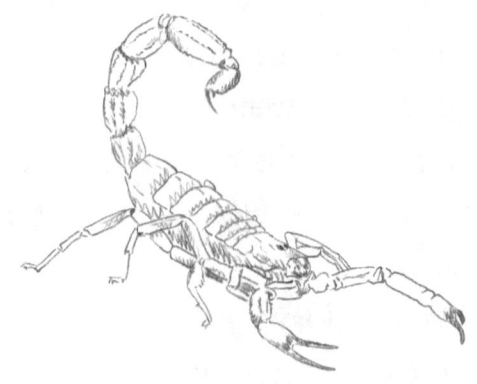

CHAPTER XXVI
The Settling of Scores
1882

inco de Mayo is a Mexican national holiday celebrating victory over the French forces of Emperor Maximilian at the Battle of Puebla in 1862. Even beyond the borders of Mexico, those of us of Mexican heritage never fail to observe this sacred occasion. Tequila flows freely, and sometimes the festivities do get out of hand. Such was the case in Tombstone in 1882.

A vaquero by the name of *Antonio Figueroa* had been drinking heavily all day. In the early evening, Deputy City Marshal Joe Poynton encountered Figueroa, blind drunk, staggering down the street, firing off his pistols in every direction with no regard for where his bullets might hit. Poynton attempted to disarm Figueroa and was shot down in the street. Happily, Poynton's wounds proved not to be fatal.

City Marshal Dave Neagle came running and ordered Figueroa to drop his weapons. Instead of complying, Figueroa turned and ran away. Neagle fired one shot, dropping Figueroa, killing him instantly.

Some in Tombstone blamed the marshal for shooting the fleeing man in the back. Quite possibly, Neagle could have apprehended Figueroa without killing him. But remember, Figueroa had already shot one person and might at the next moment have shot another. To my thinking, the situation demanded immediate decisive action. I, therefore, do not fault the marshal.

Three weeks after that shooting, Tombstone suffered another devastating fire. I happened to be in town that day, and in the confusion and chaos, I managed to begin evening the score I had to settle with the cowboys that had crippled my father.

I had ridden to Tombstone to place ads in both newspapers for some unbroken mustangs I wanted to sell. Approaching the city limits, I saw the smoke and knew immediately that this was going to be another major disaster. I urged Calcetín to a gallop, intending to volunteer my services to Marshal Neagle in helping to evacuate residents in the path of the flames. But when I spotted Hank Swilling in an alleyway, trying to catch his spooked horse, I turned to go after the man. I do not know whether he was armed or not.

I was certainly armed, for I had not yet had any opportunity to check my Colt, as required by city ordinance. Drawing my weapon, I attempted to ride Swilling down. At the last moment, he saw me and ducked behind Spangenberg's Gun Shop and Hardware Store. I wheeled Calcetín to the right and pursued Swilling toward the back entrance of the Cosmopolitan Hotel, which was already engulfed in flames. As I took aim, Swilling disappeared into the burning building. At that very instant, the entire structure collapsed. *Good riddance,* I said to myself, holstering my gun. I then went to seek out the marshal to offer my assistance in dealing with the various threats posed by the fire.

I later told Papa about my having driven Hank Swilling into a burning building, but until now, I have told no one else. I pray, Dear Reader, that I can count on your discretion.

Swilling's charred body, discovered the following day in the rubble, was never identified. His was the only life lost that day, but half the business district (the half spared the year before) was lost to the conflagration. Rebuilding began immediately.

The Bilickes, however, decided not to rebuild the Cosmopolitan Hotel. Nor did Buckskin Frank Leslie rebuild the Cosmopolitan Saloon. The Bilickes left Tombstone for California, and Mr Leslie took a job tending bar at the Oriental.

He also started drinking rather heavily, and I began to see in him a mean streak that I had never before suspected. Accusations of attempted claim jumping and attempted murder were made against him.

"Mr Leslie," I told him one day, after witnessing his beating a man nearly to death, "strong drink is going to be your undoing. I urge you to stop before it's too late."

He laughed at my concern for him. "So you've become a Prohibitionist, have you, Gaby?"

"Certainly not," I assured him. "I was baptized a Catholic, and I'll be buried a Catholic. It would kill my father were I to convert."

On the evening of July 20, yet another fire broke out, this one in the New Orleans Restaurant at the corner of Fourth and Toughnut Streets. The fire house of the Tombstone Hook and Ladder Company was next door. Both buildings were a total loss. And yet, the flames were extinguished before they could spread any further. Tombstone's volunteer fire fighters, it seems, had, by this time, become quite proficient at their jobs.

But allow me, please, to back up a week. On July 13, I had occasion to further even the score against our enemies. Entirely on my own, I was traveling from Maley to Los Neri in order to visit my brother Horace. He had written to me that he now had a sweetheart. I was anxious to hear all about her, and hopefully to meet her. Horace was thirteen and a half years of age. I was barely two months younger.

I had gone to Maley to press someone for money owed us, and I was riding Papa's stallion Nube de Truenos. I had not planned to visit Horace, but having successfully completed my business in Maley earlier than expected, I made a spur-of-the-moment decision.

Passing through West Turkey Creek Valley, I spied a riderless horse with a pair of boots hanging on the saddle horn. I seized the trailing reins and led the horse as I backtracked it in order to return it to its owner.

On the trail at night, it is common practice to hang one's boots on one's saddle horn to prevent scorpions from crawling into them. Obviously, this horse had broken free and strayed away from a campsite whilst its owner slept. Someone would be very grateful to get his boots and horse back.

I soon came to a campsite in a clearing surrounded by heavy brush. Smoke rose from a small fire, at the edge of which a coffee pot stood on hot stones. The aroma of fresh coffee filled the air, but no one seemed to be about. No doubt, the horse's owner was out looking for his horse. I tied Nube and the other horse to a bush and helped myself to a cup of coffee. I deserved it for returning the man's horse and boots. No need to wait for my host to return. As soon as I had finished my coffee, I'd be on my way.

"Little Durango, what a pleasant surprise!" The voice was that of Johnny Ringo, and he was directly behind me.

Before I could react, I heard the sound of a revolver's being cocked. I froze.

"Turn around slowly."

I did so. "Mind if I finish my coffee?" I asked.

"No, of course not. I do owe you for returning my horse. I must have chased that damned critter ten miles in my sock feet. Where's yer Paw?"

"He's around," I lied.

Ringo laughed. "Nice try. I heard he was all crippled up. I guess you must be the man of the family now."

I knew what was in store for me. I clearly remembered what road agents had done to Dahteste all those years ago. Assuming that I should shortly be relieved of my sidearm, I began calculating how to get my hand on my Derringer without alerting Ringo to what I was doing.

Off to my left, a horse whinnied. Another answered from the opposite direction.

"That'll be Papa and Mr Dodge," I said.

In truth, I had no idea who might be approaching, but then again, neither did Ringo. Nervously, he glanced to his left. The instant his eyes were off me, I dropped the cup and reached for my Colt. Firing from the hip without actually aiming, I hit Ringo in the right temple, for his head was still turned to see who was coming. Ringo dropped down dead at my feet just as Buckskin Frank Leslie, leading his horse, stepped into the clearing.

"Well done, Gaby!" said Mr Leslie. "I can see that nobody will ever have to rescue you."

"Someone else is coming," I told him, nodding to my left.

"Go on. Get out of here," he said. "I'll deal with whomever it is."

My shot had spooked Ringo's horse, which had pulled free and run away again. Nube, well trained to tolerate the sound of gunfire, stood calmly waiting where I had tied him. As I climbed into the saddle, I heard voices from the clearing behind me.

"What the fuck, Frank? Why'd you do it?" That was Billy Claiborne's voice, I was nearly certain.

"Turn your sorry ass around and get out of here before I give you some of the same," I heard Mr Leslie reply.

I later read in the newspaper that a coroner's jury had ruled Ringo's death a suicide. Apparently, Billy had not come forward as a witness.

Also from the newspaper, I learned that Pony Diehl had been arrested in New Mexico Territory and sentenced to prison for rustling cattle. His was the last name on my list.

CHAPTER XXVII
Papa's New Occupation
1882

I had always looked up to my father as a man of character and integrity. Partially crippled now and unable to ride, he nevertheless maintained his pleasant nature. He refused to become despondent or grouchy. He held on firmly to his sense of humor. And he worked out for himself a new occupation. He became a carpenter.

Indeed, Papa seemed to have an incredible facility for working with wood. He began by repairing and improving the main ranch house. He built a two-room addition for Modesta and me. He then set about to fill the house with new furniture: tables, chairs, benches, bed frames, cabinets, chests of drawers, and a dry sink. When Marietta announced that she was pregnant, Papa crafted a beautifully ornamented cradle for the expected addition to our household.

As Papa's skill developed, he acquired a county-wide reputation for quality workmanship. His handiwork was much admired. Eventually, he began accepting orders for custom pieces. Marietta saw to it that he was paid top dollar, for she was a shrewd businesswoman. Papa, on the other hand, would have given his creations away to anyone that asked.

We were still poor, of course, but we lived well, and we enjoyed one another's company. Every evening we read aloud together, adventure stories being the favorite genre of us three women. Papa still preferred poetry and philosophy, I think, but we females, outnumbering him, usually prevailed.

Anyway, I believe that he enjoyed *Ivanhoe* and *The Talisman* far more than he cared to admit.

As I compose this narrative, I find myself referring constantly to my diaries. I think I mentioned this once before, did I not? Most of my diary entries for the latter half of 1882 concern events about which I knew only what was in the newspapers. I was neither a participant in nor a first-hand witness to these goings-on. Only because they seem to me to be of historic importance, I shall include them here, and only with the sketchiest of details.

In July of 1882, Crawley Dake was replaced as US marshal for Arizona Territory by Zara T Tidbal.

That same month (July 17, to be precise), troops of the Third and Sixth Cavalry Regiments engaged warriors of White Mountain Apaches at Big Dry Fork. This was the last major engagement of the uprising that had begun at Cibecue Creek the previous year.

On November 14, Billy the Kid Claiborne challenged Buckskin Frank Leslie to a gunfight in the Oriental Saloon. They met in the street out front, and Leslie killed Claiborne, whose dying words were to the effect that Leslie had killed Johnny Ringo. "I seen him do it."

The very next day, Republican Jerome L Ward was elected sheriff of Cochise County, defeating Tombstone City Marshal Dave Neagle, who ran as an independent. Democrat Johnny Behan, strongly suspected of fraud involving public funds, had earlier dropped out of the race and left Tombstone.

In December, after surviving two attempts on his life, John Clum, who had consistently supported the Earps, sold his newspaper and left Tombstone to settle in Washington, DC, where his son and parents lived.

At about that same time, Milt Joyce sold his share of the Oriental Saloon, and in partnership with Frank Leslie, established Magnolia Ranch near the Swisshelm Mountains some nineteen miles outside Tombstone.

CHAPTER XXVIII
María Valentina Falcón
1883

On January 3, I celebrated my fourteenth birthday. Then, on February 14, I got a new baby sister: María Valentina Falcón. And god, what a sweet, dear, pretty baby she was! She had a full head of curly black hair and beautiful brown eyes with long lashes. I was totally enchanted with her, as, of course, were her parents and her grandmother. We called her *Val* for short.

In March, our entire household traveled south to the village of Cananea, Sonora, a mining community in northern Mexico, where we spent a few days with Modesta's parents (Marietta's grandparents). From there we traveled east to Los Neri to visit Horace and my Neri relatives.

Horace was especially smitten with his new baby sister. I had known that he would be.

Miss Nellie, by the way, abode at the ranch during our absence, tending to our livestock and looking after our kitchen garden. What a good friend she was to us!

Pete Spence had not been heard of for more than a year. We had speculated amongst ourselves that perhaps he might be dead. Of course, Pete would have been afraid of Papa, but it seemed strange that he had not attempted some reprisal against Marietta for her testifying against him.

Then in July, we read in the newspaper that Pete had been convicted of manslaughter and sentenced to five years in prison. It seems that Pete had left Tombstone to become a deputy sheriff in Georgetown, New Mexico Territory, where, in June, he had pistol-whipped a man to death.

"At least, we don't have to worry about his showing up around here anytime soon," Modesta sighed.

As things turned out, Pete spent only eighteen months in prison before receiving a full pardon. He returned to Arizona Territory, where, in partnership with Phineas Clanton, he would one day establish, just south of Globe City, a goat ranch very like our own. He did not give us any trouble. We never even saw him again. I suppose he finally decided to go straight.

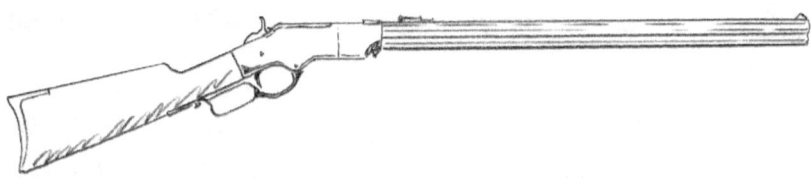

CHAPTER XXIX
THE BISBEE RAID
1883 - 1884

In the early evening of December 8, 1883, five outlaws raided the Goldwater and Castañeda General Store in Bisbee. There being, at that time, no bank in Bisbee, payroll for the Copper Queen Mine was usually held in this store's safe. The outlaws expected to ride away with at least seven thousand dollars, but their timing was poor. The payroll had not yet arrived.

Whilst four masked men stood guard outside, their leader Tex Howard stepped inside without a mask. Drawing his weapon, he demanded that the safe be opened. The safe, however, contained only eight hundred dollars. Or perhaps there was a much as three thousand. Different witnesses have named different amounts. It is hard to know the truth. But the mine payroll was missing. That much is certain.

In any event, whilst Howard was inside the store, several citizens became aware that a holdup was in progress. When shooting broke out in the street, four people were killed. They were JC Tappenier, John A Nolly (a teamster), Cochise County Deputy Sheriff Tom Smith, and Annie Roberts (owner of the Bisbee House Restaurant). Mrs Roberts was pregnant. One other man known only as *Indian Joe* suffered a leg wound. Initially, the robbers escaped.

The Copper Queen Mine posted a two thousand dollar reward for the capture of the outlaws. Deputy Sheriff Billy Daniels organized a posse, deputizing several civilians, including gambler Henry Frost, Nathan Waite, and John Heath.

Waite and Heath together owned a dance hall in Bisbee.

The posse followed the robbers' trail far into the wilderness. When tracks indicated that the outlaws had split up, the posse split up too, with Heath, Waite, and Frost following two of the outlaws and the rest of the posse following the other three. Both trails eventually went cold.

Sheriff Ward being away from Tombstone on official business, Undersheriff Wallace rode to Bisbee and took charge of the investigation. In spite of the masks they had worn, Tex Howard's four companions in crime, it transpired, had been recognized as Big Dan Dowd, Red Sample, Billy Delaney, and York Kelly.

Howard and Sample were later apprehended in Clifton, Arizona Territory. Dowd and Delaney were captured in Sonora by *tío* Felipe's *rurales*. Claiming the reward, *tío* promptly turned the two men over to Sheriff Ward in Tombstone. There was no extradition hearing. The last to be taken was York Kelly, who was apprehended at Deming, New Mexico Territory.

Also charged was John Heath, who had been part of the posse that had pursued the robbers immediately after the hold-up. It seems that Heath, a known associate of the other five, had a criminal record that included cattle rustling, robbery, and burglary. There was additional evidence as well, I believe, but I did not attend the trial and so cannot say how strong that evidence was.

Sentenced to hang were Tex Howard, Big Dan Dowd, Red Sample, Billy Delaney, and York Kelly. Heath, tried separately, was given a sentence of life in prison. The entire county was outraged that the organizer of this atrocity had received such leniency.

On February 22, a lynch mob made up of miners (mostly Cornishmen) overpowered and disarmed the sheriff, dragged Heath from his cell, and hanged him from a telephone pole. The other five outlaws, already awaiting execution, were left in their cells.

The coroner's report issued by Dr Goodfellow, who had witnessed the lynching, concluded that Heath had died from "emphysema of the lungs, which might have been, and probably was, caused by strangulation, self-inflicted or otherwise, as in accordance with the medical evidence."

The following month, sentence on Howard, Dowd, Delaney, Kelly, and Sample was carried out by the sheriff. Local entrepreneurs erected a grandstand just outside the jail yard, meaning to sell tickets at a dollar fifty each to watch the first "legal" hanging in Cochise County.

Miss Nellie was outraged and protested strongly and loudly to Sheriff Ward, but to no avail. He refused to intervene. And so Miss Nellie hired a gang of men with axes to destroy the grandstand the night before the execution. Even so, more than a thousand people witnessed the grim event, but no one profited from it.

And still, the saga of the Bisbee Raid was not complete. In the days leading up to the execution, Miss Nellie chanced to overhear a rumor that a medical school in another part of the country had sent men to carry out a secret midnight exhumation of the bodies of the five outlaws. She, therefore, hired her own crew armed with clubs to stand guard night and day over the graves for more than a week.

CHAPTER XXX
SAN BERNARDINO RANCH
1884

When Fanny Cunningham finally lost her battle with tuberculosis, her five children came to live with their aunt Miss Nellie in Tombstone.

At about that same time, Mr Slaughter expanded his ranching operation by buying sixty-five thousand of the original seventy-three thousand acres of the San Bernardino Ranch (formerly known as *Rancho San Bernardino*) from the estate of my ancestor Ignacio Perez. Quite suddenly, I came into a great deal of money: almost eight thousand dollars, approximately one tenth of the purchase price, other relatives, whom I had never even met, receiving the rest. I have no clue as to the ultimate disposition of the other eight thousand acres.

I immediately bought new tools and materials for Papa's woodworking. Then, guided by the sound advice of Papa, Mr Dodge, and Charlie Smith, I made large investments in Wells Fargo, the Copper Queen Mine, and Union Pacific Railroad. I also made smaller investments in several other enterprises. Barring a general recession and the complete collapse of the economy, I could now count on a secure income for life. I had never imagined myself in such an enviable position. It felt almost as if I had somehow cheated. I had to remind myself again and again that I had done nothing wrong.

But let me tell you what I now know about the San Bernardino Ranch. About one third of its acreage lies in Arizona Territory, specifically in the southeast corner of Cochise County, which occupies the southeast corner of Arizona Territory. The other two thirds of the ranch are in Mexico. In 1822, when Ignacio Perez purchased the *rancho* from the original land-grant holder, he paid only ninety pesos for it. Near the western edge of San Bernardino Ranch is Los Neri.

Within a year after Mr Slaughter's acquiring San Bernardino Ranch, Henry Hooker would begin buying up other ranches in Cochise and Graham Counties. His original Sierra Bonita Ranch, by the way, is in Cochise County but far to the north of San Bernardino Ranch and ever so slightly to the west.

I suppose I should try to draw you a map. I'm sure that my narrative would make more sense if you could see the relationships of all the places I mention.

In November of 1884, Fred Dodge was elected constable of a justice precinct roughly coextensive with the City of Tombstone. I absolutely do not understand why we have to have so many overlapping jurisdictions. I suppose this system must make sense to somebody; else it never would have been set up this way. But it makes no sense to me.

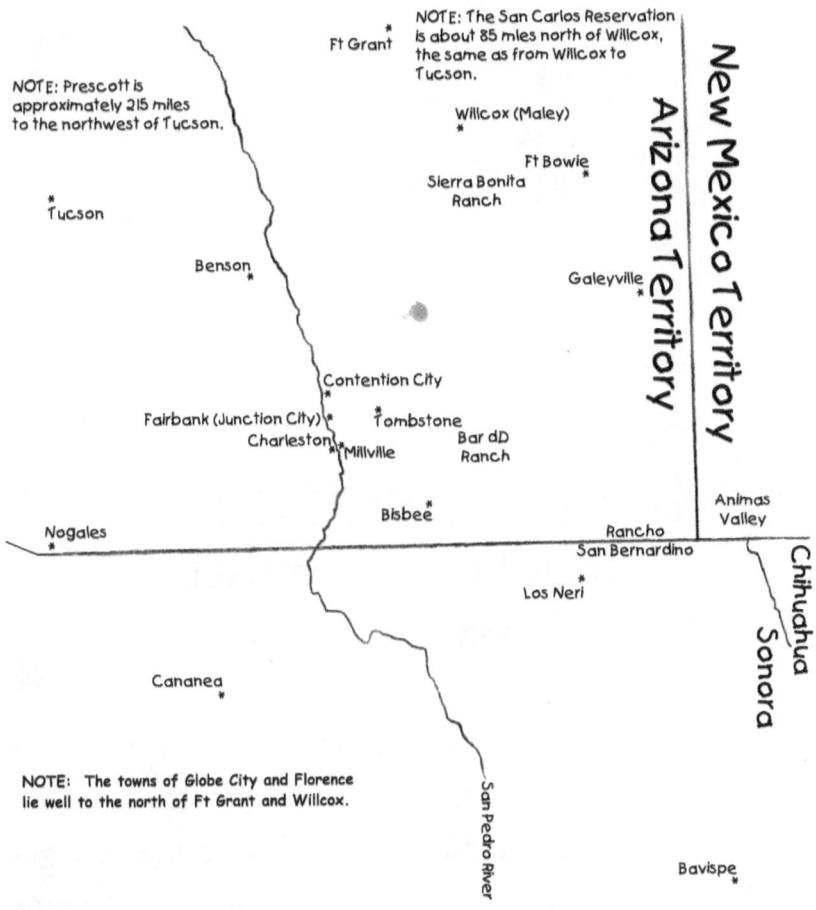

NOTE: The San Carlos Reservation is about 85 miles north of Willcox, the same as from Willcox to Tucson.

NOTE: Prescott is approximately 215 miles to the northwest of Tucson.

Ft Grant

Willcox (Maley)

Ft Bowie

Sierra Bonita Ranch

Tucson

Benson

Galeyville

Arizona Territory

New Mexico Territory

Contention City

Fairbank (Junction City)

Tombstone

Charleston

Millville

Bar dD Ranch

Bisbee

Animas Valley

Nogales

Rancho San Bernardino

Los Neri

Chihuahua

Sonora

Cananea

NOTE: The towns of Globe City and Florence lie well to the north of Ft Grant and Willcox.

San Pedro River

Bavispe

CHAPTER XXXI
MR A FRANK RANDALL
1885 - 1886

The partnership between Frank Leslie and Milt Joyce endured for only a few months. When the two men had a falling out, Mr Leslie bought Milt Joyce's interest in Magnolia Ranch and became the sole owner.

In May, Geronimo made his third breakout from the reservation, the previous breakouts having occurred in August of 1878 and in September of 1881. When the army began taking on extra scouts, Mr Leslie signed up. I suppose he needed the income to help support his ranch; however, he only stayed on the job for a month before he was dismissed for drunkenness.

I was sixteen years old now and thirsty for adventure. I informed Papa that I too intended to sign up to scout for the army, as Mr Leslie had done.

"And what makes you think the army would hire you?"

"Why wouldn't they?" I demanded. "I can do anything any other scout can do, and probably better than most."

"I'm sure that's true, Gaby, but I've never heard of the army's using female scouts. It simply isn't done."

"Ha!" I crowed. "That's where you're wrong, Papa. Didn't you ever hear of Calamity Jane? When General Crook was waging the Black Hills War, she was one of his most trusted scouts. And now he's here in Arizona Territory chasing Geronimo. When he sees how well I can ride and track and shoot, you can bet he'll hire me."

Papa seemed genuinely surprised to learn that General Crook had ever employed a female scout. I'm not sure he even believed me until I produced an old issue of *Frank Leslie's Illustrated Newspaper* and showed him the article about Martha Jane Cannary, otherwise known as *Calamity Jane.* There was even a picture of her in buckskins.

Wisely, Papa resisted his instinct to forbid me to do what I had already made my mind up to do. Instead, he simply begged me to postpone my leaving home. "Stick around until after your next birthday. Then, if you are still determined to do this, I'll give you my full support."

Reluctantly, I agreed. I simply could not bear to refuse my father his one request, even though I felt it to be totally unreasonable.

On November 25, Deputy Sheriff Charles Smith was involved in a violent altercation at the Bank Exchange Bar in Tombstone. Although un-armed at the time, Smith attempted to break up a fight, only to have one of the belligerents, Charley Cunningham, turn on him.

"You damned harelip son-of-a-bitch!" Cunningham shouted as he charged at Smith.

Deputy US Marshal Dick Gage was standing nearby and offered Smith one of his revolvers. Smith fired, wounding Cunningham in the leg.

A grand jury refused to indict Smith, who, after all, was only defending himself. But Cunningham bore a grudge and would eventually seek revenge.

When my seventeenth birthday rolled around, I had neither forgotten nor forsaken my ambition to scout for General Crook, but before taking my leave of the ranch, I had to know that everything was running so smoothly that I should scarcely be missed. Throughout the winter, one minor crisis after another arose, and I dealt patiently with each.

Finally, I realized that there was no longer anything holding me back. I was free to depart. When I informed Papa that I was ready to leave, he gave me his Sharps long-range rifle and some quite-unnecessary advice.

"If you meet up with Indians on the trail," Papa told me, "it's a friendly gesture to offer a gift of tobacco. So buy some at your first opportunity, and always keep it handy."

"I'll do that, Papa. Thank you."

I hugged everyone *goodbye* and kissed my little sister Val (now three years old), then mounted Nube and rode away.

At Fort Bowie, I was disappointed to be told that the army had no need of my services. But then Mr A Frank Randall, an itinerant photographer, hired me to guide him deep into Apachería for the purpose of making photographic portraits of the Indians.

The Apache nation was now at peace. Only a few small bands of renegades remained defiant. General Crook expected shortly to bring in these last holdouts, including Geronimo.

Mr Randall and I visited several remote communities on the San Carlos Reservation before moving on to the Fort Apache Reservation. At the village of Cochise, I asked after my friend Dahteste and learned that she had joined Geronimo in revolt.

Now, I was glad that I had not become a scout, for as such, I should be Dahteste's enemy. My job would be to help apprehend her.

As Mr Randall's assistant, I was no one's enemy. Instead, I was learning everything there was to know about photography. Already, Mr Randall trusted me, entirely on my own, to develop his glass plates. I was even allowed to take a few pictures myself from time to time. I had never, in my entire life, been happier.

Upon our return to Fort Bowie, we were astonished to learn that General Crook had been relieved of command and General Nelson Miles had replaced him. General Crook was a remarkably competent officer. What had he done, I wondered, to be so humiliated?

Paid up in full, I took my leave of Mr Randall and began trying to learn how General Crook had so suddenly fallen into disgrace. For the most part, my questions went unanswered until I met a young lieutenant known to the Apaches as *Nantan Bse-che* (*Chief Big Nose*). His real name was *Charles Bare Gatewood*. Speaking in the Apache tongue, of which he had a fair command, he told me everything, and no one overhearing us could have guessed of what we were speaking.

"General Crook and I did not always see eye to eye regarding treatment of Indians on the reservations, but in pursuit of broncos, he made good use of Apache scouts," Gatewood told me.

"*Broncos?*" I asked. It was a term I had only ever heard applied to horses.

"Renegade Apaches that break out from the reservation: *broncos* is how the army calls them. In any case, our own Apache scouts know the mountains of northern Mexico as well as do the broncos that make those mountains their base from which to stage raids in Texas, Arizona Territory, and New Mexico Territory. With official permission from Mexico to pursue breakout Apaches across the border, Crook so successfully harried the renegades that, in March, Geronimo agreed to sit down with General Crook to discuss terms of surrender. The meeting took place in Mexico at Cañon de los Embudos. Terms were agreed to, and the official surrender was to take place on the morrow, but in the night, the Apaches slipped away."

"Why?" I asked. "What happened?"

"A soldier, it seems, making mischief, told one of the Apaches that, as soon as they had turned over their weapons, they'd all be shot or hanged. Apparently, they believed him."

"But that wasn't General Crook's fault," I objected.

"No," he agreed, "but that's not how the army sees it. When you are in command, you are ultimately responsible for everything that happens."

"Excuse me, Lieutenant," interrupted a smartly uniformed sergeant major, saluting crisply, "The general would like a word with the young lady."

"With me?" I asked.

"Yes, ma'am," answered the sergeant major, "if that would not be too inconvenient."

"Carry on," said Lieutenant Gatewood. "You mustn't keep the general waiting."

I followed the sergeant major back to the same building where I had been interviewed for a scouting position some weeks earlier. The very same colonel that had turned down my application before now showed me into General Miles's office.

"I overheard you conversing with Lieutenant Gatewood in the Apache tongue. I understand from the colonel here that you once applied to scout for the army."

"I did indeed, sir, but I've changed my mind. That is no longer my ambition."

"May I ask why?"

I shrugged. I was, at first, reluctant to tell him my reason, but then decided that to do so could cause no one any harm. "I have learned that a childhood friend of mine, someone very dear to my heart, is with Geronimo. I could not bear to become her enemy."

"I can appreciate that sentiment," said the general. "Perhaps you'd consider a non-combat rôle. We badly need translators. As such, you could help bring this conflict to an end before casualties on both sides mount any higher."

I only needed a moment to consider this offer before accepting.

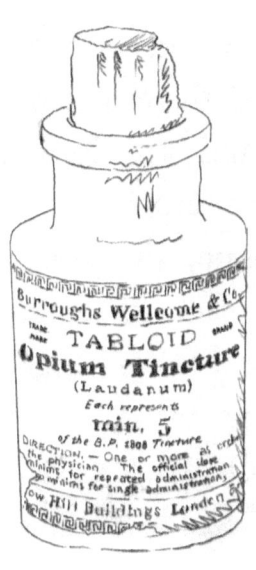

CHAPTER XXXII
SURRENDER AT GUADALUPE CANYON
1886

Lieutenant Gatewood was not in good health. What exactly afflicted him was never clear to me, but he endured constant pain, which occasionally became so intense that he was forced to seek the nominal relief that a small dose of laudanum afforded him. He was always careful not to over-use the substance, lest he become addicted to it, as so many others had done.

General Miles had inherited Gatewood from his predecessor, and therefore, did not initially trust him overmuch. And yet, because Gatewood spoke the Apache language and had once been on friendly terms with Geronimo, the general decided to send Gatewood as his personal emissary to Geronimo. Other troops were already scouring Chihuahua and Sonora with orders to seek out and destroy the renegade bands. Only by surrendering immediately to General Miles could Geronimo hope to avoid annihilation.

On August 24, Lieutenant Gatewood, backed up by only two soldiers, two interpreters, and two Apache scouts, entered Geronimo's camp and opened the discussion by offering a gift of tobacco (fifteen pounds). The interpreters were Tom Horn and Jesús María Yestes. I should have liked to have been there myself, but General Miles kept me with him.

On September 2, Geronimo's band, accompanied by Lieutenant Gatewood's party, arrived at Guadalupe Canyon. The following day, General Miles arrived. I was, of course, in the general's entourage. We were joined later that day by Mr

Slaughter, who had come to witness the big event. The site, after all, was on his land, Guadalupe Canyon being part of San Bernardino Ranch. The surrender was formally concluded on September 4.

During the days that we were camped in Guadalupe Canyon, I had occasion to visit privately with Dahteste and Gouyen, both of whom had surrendered with Geronimo. They introduced me to a third woman, Lozen, who looked to be a generation older than Gouyen and Dahteste. Lozen, I later learned, had been Geronimo's chief tactician. She had also served as shaman for the little band, which numbered between thirty and forty.

I gave the three women all the tobacco I carried and as much coffee as I felt I could spare. We chatted amiably, and Dahteste recounted for Gouyen and Lozen how I, at age seven, had shot the two men that were assaulting her. "I called her *Little Mankiller*. She is my friend, and I am hers. Nothing will ever change that."

The Apaches were under the impression that they would soon be returning to the San Carlos Reservation. Instead, they were to be imprisoned in Florida for an indefinite period of time. There had already been one too many breakouts. The army was taking no chance of there ever being another. In fact, at General Miles's insistence, all Chiricahuas, even those that had never left the reservation, were now arrested and sent east as prisoners of war.

I was beside myself with rage but helpless to do anything about it.

CHAPTER XXXIII
A New Sheriff in Tombstone
1886 - 1887

The November election made cattleman John Slaughter the new sheriff of Cochise County. His in-laws, the Howells, were to run the San Bernardino Ranch in his absence.

The power of the Ten Percent Ring had been broken, and the Clanton Mob was in disarray, but the Arizona Borderlands were still crime-infested enough to keep a conscientious lawman busy day and night. The Tombstone jailhouse soon became known as *Hotel Slaughter.*

Sheriff Slaughter wore a pearl-handled .44 in a cross-draw holster and carried a ten-gauge repeating shotgun about with him at all times. His name for the shotgun was the *Equalizer*.

Taking advantage of the fact that Sheriff Slaughter was of the mistaken belief that I had been an army scout, I asked him to make me a deputy sheriff.

"I can't do that, Gaby. I'm too beholden to your father to risk getting you killed."

"I'm not a child to be protected," I countered. "I'm full grown and I can take care of myself as well as anyone ever can. Also, I'm honest, and that is not as common a quality as it ought to be."

"I know. But there's also this to consider. If I were to pin a badge on a little slip of a girl like you, my credibility would be shot to hell. I'm planning to run again, you know. I don't enjoy the luxury of being just a lawman. I have to be a politician, too."

I tried one more argument, even though I figured it was pointless to do so. "I'm the best tracker in the territory. And the best shot. If you're serious about this job, you're going to need someone with skills like mine to back you up."

"I'll tell you what," he said. "The first time I need a first-rate tracker, I'll send for you."

"Promise?"

"I do. I promise."

My former schoolmate Burt Alford—the boy with whom I had skipped school on the day of the big shootout between the Earps and the cowboys—also applied for a deputy's position and was hired immediately. Other deputies hired by Sheriff Slaughter included Jeff Milton, who, in later years, would become famous as a railroad detective, and Cesario Lucero. Harelip Charlie Smith, who had served under Sheriffs Behan, Ward, and Hatch, was still on the job.

Johnny Behan, by the way, in 1887, became superintendent of Yuma Territorial Prison. I had assumed that his career in public service was over. I had heard not a word about him in more than four years, but apparently, he was still well connected.

During this period, Cochise County suffered a spate of train robberies. Amongst the most violent of outlaws specializing in railroad holdups was the Jack Taylor Gang, which operated in Sonora as well as in Arizona Territory. Felipe Neri, my *tío*, was as anxious to capture the Jack Taylor Gang as was Sheriff Slaughter.

It was, in fact, in aid of apprehending members of this murderous gang that I was first called upon as a tracker. It was almost midnight when Deputy Smith arrived at the ranch to ask for my help. As he led me back to where Sheriff Slaughter and other deputies waited, Smith filled me in on the situation.

"We got a tip earlier today that Nieves Deron, Geronimo Miranda, Manuel Robles, and Fred Federico were hiding out at a farmhouse belonging to Flora Cardenas. We rode out there, but the four men had already fled. Mrs Cardenas swears that she does not know where they might have gone. She's probably lying, but none of us had the stomach for beating the truth out of her."

"I should hope not," I said, horrified by the very suggestion.

Smith laughed at my squeamishness. "We were able to track them ourselves for a ways, but the trail got harder and harder to pick out. Eventually, we lost the trail completely, and the sheriff sent me to fetch you. Are you really as good as he hopes you are?"

"I am," I said, "but if the trail is as hard to see as you say, we may have to wait till morning. An easy trail I can follow by starlight, but for a difficult trail, I need more light."

"Yeah, we figured that," Smith said. "The others have made camp for the night. They'll have coffee waiting for us."

"There's just one thing," I said. "If I'm going to do this, I want a badge. I'll give it back when the job is done."

"A badge is really important to you, is it?" Smith asked.

"Essential," I said firmly. "I can find those men for you, wherever they have gone, but not without a badge."

Demanding a badge was silly of me, I know, but I had so wanted to be a deputy sheriff, and wearing an official badge, even for a few hours, would allow me to believe (or at least pretend to believe) that I had finally achieved my ambition.

"Fair enough," said Smith, unpinning the badge on his own jacket front and passing it to me.

Later, as I dismounted at the posse's overnight camp, Sheriff Slaughter raised an eyebrow, but said nothing about the fact that I was wearing a deputy's badge on my jacket front.

Lucero, smiling broadly, asked me, "Shall I pour you a cup of coffee, deputy?"

"Thank you," I said. "I surely could use some coffee."

From what Smith had told me the night before, I had expected the outlaws' trail to be a lot more difficult to follow than I found it to be. In less than an hour, I led the posse to the home of a woodcutter named *Guadeloupe Robles* on the outskirts of Contention City. As it would later be learned, this Guadaloupe Robles was the brother of Manuel Robles. Concealed by a stand of juniper trees, we watched the house long enough to determine that only two of the wanted men—Manuel Robles and Nieves Deron—were still there with their host Guadaloupe Robles.

To Smith and Lucero, Sheriff Slaughter said, "You two go around back. Burt, you take up a position near the corral. Don't let them get to their horses. Jeff and I'll go in the front."

"What about me?" I asked. "I want to help."

"You stay right here with the horses. Keep your eyes open and your gun ready. We wouldn't want them to escape on our own mounts."

After giving Lucero and Smith time to get into position, Sheriff Slaughter crashed through the front door with Deputy Milton right behind him. Gunfire erupted and two men came tumbling out the front windows, gathered themselves up, and ran toward some enormous rocks on the side of the house away from the corral.

I had a clear shot and fired. One man—Manuel Robles, I later learned—went down. But before I could fire at the other man—Nieves Deron—Sheriff Slaughter and Deputy Milton came running out of the house and into my field of fire.

They quickly brought Deron down, but as they did so, the wounded Robles managed to crawl into the shelter of the rocks. We searched for him there, found traces of blood, but the man himself had disappeared completely.

Deron was dead, as was Guadaloupe Robles inside the house. Sheriff Slaughter had been nicked in the ear by a bullet.

I tracked the other two outlaws from the house to a freight siding, where they had apparently boarded a train with their mounts. Sheriff Slaughter wired ahead, but to no avail.

A week or so later, *tío* Felipe's *rurales* captured the gang's leader Jack Taylor, who was subsequently sentenced in Sonora to life in prison. Not many days after that in the Sierra Madre Occidental, *rurales* engaged Manuel Robles and Geronimo Miranda in a gun battle and killed them both.

The *rurales*, it seems to me, are Mexico's version of the Texas Rangers. They are organized in much the same way, operate in a similar fashion, and enjoy a like success rate.

Fred Federico was the only gang member still at large. More than a year later (on September 12, 1888), he would ambush and kill Deputy Lucero (mistaking him for Sheriff Slaughter), only to be captured before making his getaway. He would be tried, convicted, and hanged in Tombstone.

Ike Clanton, meanwhile, had formed a new outlaw gang consisting of Lee Renfro, Kid Swingle, Longhair Sprague, Billy Evans, and Ike's brother-in-law Elwin Stanley. On June 1, 1887, Range Detective Jonas V Brighton attempted to arrest Ike for cattle rustling. Ike resisted and was killed.

Ike's brother Phineas was convicted of grand larceny and cattle rustling and sentenced to ten years. He would serve but seventeen months. It would be after his early release that he and Pete Spence would form a partnership to start their goat-ranching operation.

This same year, 1887, May Evans divorced Frank Leslie, charging physical cruelty and adultery. She was awarded six hundred dollars and one quarter interest in Magnolia Ranch. Mr Leslie was ordered by Judge William H Barnes to pay all legal fees and court costs.

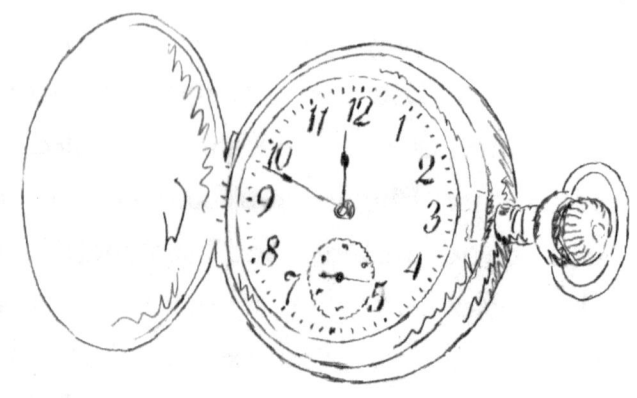

CHAPTER XXXIV
THE BAVISPE EARTHQUAKE
1887

Before relating what I recall of the Bavispe earthquake, I feel that I must tell you a bit more about George Emory Goodfellow, whom I have mentioned several times before. Indeed, you have probably surmised by now that I quite idolize the good doctor. A polymath, a skilled surgeon, and a great humanitarian, he is probably the bravest and most heroic person I have ever encountered.

Once, when a Tombstone mine caved in, Dr Goodfellow was amongst the first rescuers to descend into the murky depths. At great risk to himself, he treated the injured miners on the spot before helping to carry them back to the surface.

During the great fire of 1881, a volunteer firefighter was badly injured by falling debris that destroyed his face. Dr Goodfellow devised a method of reconstructive surgery that gave the man his looks back. Nor did the doctor charge for this service, as the man had been injured whilst working without pay for the benefit of the community.

Dr Goodfellow pioneered a number of surgical procedures that have since become standard medical practice. He was one of the first surgeons known to use spinal anesthesia. This he did by dissolving cocaine in the patient's own spinal fluid and then re-injecting it.

Mind you, Dr Goodfellow was no saint. He drank to excess, he gambled, and he frequently sought out the company of prostitutes. But I don't hold any of that against him. That's just the way men are.

Dr Goodfellow was a founding member of the Tombstone Club, a posh gentlemen's club on the upper floor of the Ritchie Building. He also helped to establish the Tombstone Scientific Society. He was a major investor in the Huachuca Water Company. I think you get the idea. Tombstone was fortunate to have such a remarkable man.

So now to the Bavispe earthquake of May 3, 1887. Bavispe was, at that time, a town of about seven hundred souls. Bavispe is located in Sonora some ninety miles to the south southeast of Tombstone. When the earth began to shake, most of the town's adobe structures crumbled. Forty people perished, and countless others were badly injured.

I happened, that day, to be in Tombstone to have Calcetín and Nube re-shod. After leaving the two horses at the farrier's shop, I went into a general store to give the storekeeper a list of supplies needed for the ranch, but he was busy filling an enormous order for Dr Goodfellow.

It was whilst I waited that I learned of the earthquake in Sonora. The goods that Dr Goodfellow was buying were for a relief effort. I immediately wrote Dr Goodfellow a check for as much as I felt I could afford.

He accepted gratefully and told the storekeeper to double his order. "I'll be back in an hour to collect it all."

As Dr Goodfellow turned to leave the store, I said to him, "If you're going to Bavispe, I'm going with you. With a wagon so heavily laden, you'll need a shotgun guard. I can do that much to help. Maybe I can even be of some use after we get there."

"Alright, but don't be late. I'm not waiting for you."

"I'll be here when you get back," I promised.

I went then to look up Mr Dodge and beg for the loan of his shotgun. "And would you try to get word to Papa that I've gone to Mexico with Dr Goodfellow. He's expecting me home this afternoon. I don't know how long I'll be gone."

On my way back to the general store, I ran into Miss Nellie, who was canvassing the business district, soliciting contributions to an earthquake-relief fund sponsored by Sacred Heart Church. I gave her all the cash I had on my person and told her that I was leaving within the hour to accompany Dr Goodfellow to Bavispe.

"I'll see you there," she said.

The devastation we found in Bavispe was infinitely worse than I could ever have imagined. The town looked as though it had been subject to a week's bombardment by heavy artillery. Not a single structure remained intact. The suffering was heartbreaking. I wanted to help, but hardly knew where to start.

"Take charge of handing out food, blankets and water," Dr Goodfellow instructed me. "I have injured to treat."

When the goods on the wagon had all been distributed, I joined a crew that was digging through the rubble in search of survivors. Most often, it was corpses that we discovered.

On our second day in Bavispe, another wagon-load of emergency supplies arrived, this one from Sacred Heart Church. Miss Nellie arrived with that wagon and immediately began organizing a field hospital, for she had nursing experience and seemed to know exactly what needed to be done.

I switched jobs to become her assistant. We saved countless lives, but I hope never again to live through such an experience. None of our efforts would have meant much but for Dr Goodfellow's heroic determination and surgical skills.

He was dubbed *El Doctor Santo* by the citizens of Sonora. Even the government in Mexico City expressed its gratitude. *Presidente* Porfirio Díaz presented Dr Goodfellow with a silver medal and a magnificent riding horse named *El Rosillo* (*The Roan*).

Later, Dr Goodfellow returned with CS Fly to document the geological effects of the earthquake. The detailed report he published was praised by the United States Geological Service.

I wish that I could close this chapter without mentioning an unfortunate incident of which I have only recently learned. But that would hardly be consistent with my stated intention of writing a "true account."

Dr Goodfellow, it seems, was expelled, in 1872, from the United States Naval Academy for violently persecuting a Black cadet, John H Conyers. It makes me sad to think that this might be true. I can only say that, in all the time I have known Dr Goodfellow, I have never once seen in him any evidence of a racist attitude. I should very much like to think that he has grown beyond such stupidity and smallness of spirit.

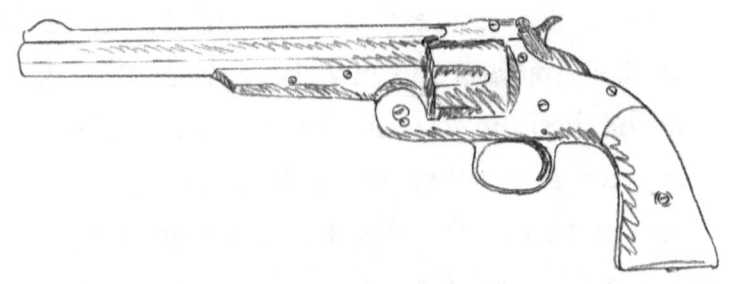

CHAPTER XXXV
THE APACHE KID
1887

I only became aware of the Apache Kid when he first became a fugitive. I have followed his story with interest ever since.

The Apache Kid's real name is *Haskay-bay-nay-ntayl*. He was born in the early 1860s to the Black Rocks People of Aravaipa Canyon, well to the south of the San Carlos Reservation. As a small child, he was captured by raiding Yuma Indians, only to be rescued a few years later by the US Cavalry.

As a homeless child, he then scavenged around army camps, eventually becoming something of a mascot to the troops. Chief of Scouts Al Sieber took a particular interest in him and began to look out for his welfare. Only later did the Apache Kid, as he had now been dubbed by the soldiers, learn that his real father was still alive.

In his teens, the Apache Kid signed up to be a scout for General Crook. He quickly rose to the rank of sergeant.

In late May of 1887, a company of Apache scouts, drunk on a home-brew called *tiswin*, fell to quarreling angrily amongst themselves. Shooting broke out and three of the scouts died. One of those killed was the Apache Kid's real father. The Apache Kid himself was accused of killing a fellow scout known as *Rip*.

On June 1, Al Sieber and Lieutenant John Pierce ordered the Apache scouts involved in the altercation to surrender their weapons and submit to arrest. The Apache Kid and the others initially complied. They allowed themselves to be disarmed and taken into custody.

A crowd of civilian onlookers had gathered. Suddenly, that crowd transformed itself into an angry mob, from which shots were fired at the scouts, one shot wounding Al Sieber by mistake. The Apache Kid and the other scouts then, fearing for their lives, fled into the wilderness.

The army sent out patrols to attempt to capture the fugitive scouts, but never even caught sight of them. Later that month, the Apache Kid found a way to send word to General Miles that he wished to surrender, but that he wanted a guarantee that he would not be shot on sight. The general so pledged, and the Apache Kid and the four others surrendered.

At court martial, they were found guilty of mutiny and sentenced to death by firing squad. That sentence was soon commuted to life in prison. General Miles intervened to reduce the sentence even further to ten years. The five then were sent to Alcatraz Island.

The following year, 1888, however, their convictions were overturned and they were released, only to be re-arrested some months later and charged again, this time by civilian authorities.

Convicted a second time, they were sentenced to seven years.

On November 2, 1889, at a spot called *Kelvin Grade,* the five scouts and four other prisoners in route from Globe City to Yuma Territorial Prison somehow managed to overpower their guards (Pinal County lawmen) and got away. In the course of this daring escape, two guards died and the driver, Eugene Middleton, was wounded.

Mr Middleton, who happens to be a casual acquaintance of Papa's through Fred Dodge, offered Papa and me the following account of the incident: "The one knowed as Pas-Lau-Tau shot and killed Glenn Reynolds with his own gun. How he got his hands on it I can't say. Deputy William Holmes just keeled over with a heart attack and died. Nobody ever laid a finger on him. Pas-Lau-Tau then pointed the gun at me and fired. I fell to the ground bleeding. That's when one of them other Apaches came up with a big rock, meaning to crush my skull, but the Kid wouldn't stand for it. I think the reason the Kid wanted to save my life was because I gave him a cigarette once. Or maybe he just don't hold with unnecessary killing. Either way, I owe him my life."

Most of the escapees were soon re-captured; not so the Apache Kid. It has now been more than ten years since the Kelvin Grade escape, and no one has yet found a single verifiable trace of him.

CHAPTER XXXVI
THE NOTORIOUS PONY DIEHL
1887 - 1888

Having learned well from Mr Randal the technical aspects of photography, I was anxious now to perfect the associated arts, particularly composition and lighting. I purchased by mail order every piece of equipment and paraphernalia I thought that I might ever require.

How exactly I meant to put photography to good use I had yet to decide. Did I want to open a portrait studio, such as the one operated by the Flys in Tombstone? Or should I find more satisfaction traveling about in a specially equipped wagon, as Mr Randal does? Every town I knew of already had a photographic studio. I doubted that any community in the territory could support two competing photographers. Finally, I decided to go with the wagon, for I was as fascinated with the possibilities of landscape photography as I was with portraiture.

I told Papa what I wanted to do and asked him if he could help me pick out a wagon and then customize it for me.

"I cannot imagine any challenge that I'd more enjoy tackling," he said.

The project took weeks to complete, but when the wagon was done and my equipment was stowed aboard, I could not have been more pleased.

"It's beautiful, Papa. Thank you with all my heart," I said, hugging him fiercely.

I then commissioned a sign-painter in Tombstone to letter on either side panel *Photography by Little Durango*. The wagon itself was dark green.

The lettering was gold outlined in black. My team consisted of two well-matched dapple-greys. The entire effect was astonishingly beautiful, almost as eye-catching as a circus wagon, but in a more tasteful way (if that doesn't sound too absurd).

For the first few weeks, I stayed pretty close to home. I made free portraits of anyone I felt comfortable imposing upon. Even Mollie Fly and Kitty allowed me to take their pictures. I photographed Papa and Marietta with five-year-old Val. I made Modesta's portrait, as well as Mr Dodge's, Deputy Smith's, Sheriff Slaughter's, Buckskin Frank Leslie's, and Burt Alford's.

I photographed townscapes and landscapes too, and with every picture I made, my skills improved and my confidence grew. Eventually, I was ready to venture further from home.

I traveled first to Los Neri, then on to El Paso, Texas. There I crossed back into Mexico, traveled south through Chihuahua and far into the state of Durango. At Ciudad Durango, I turned westward and made for Sinaloa. I went all the way to the coast before turning northward. This was the first time I had ever seen the sea. For the next few days, I hugged the coast.

How many hundreds of miles had I covered? How many hundreds of photographs had I made? Eventually, I entered southern Sonora. Since leaving Los Neri, every mile I had covered represented new country for me. I had enjoyed tremendously this meandering exploration, but now I was headed for home. I was missing my family terribly, and I was missing the Bar Double D.

At a small café in the city of Hermosillo, I encountered someone from my past.

"Little Durango," he said. "Fancy seeing you here. Mind if I sit with you?"

He did not wait for an answer but pulled out a chair and sat down opposite me.

"Pony Diehl," I said, "if I'd run into you even a year ago, I'd have shot you on sight. I thought you were in prison."

"I got out in '87, came down here to avoid more trouble."

"I hope you can manage that," I said, and I actually meant it. "Not everybody gets a second chance in life."

"Yeah, I know what you mean. A guy I used to ride with came down too, but he couldn't stay out of trouble. He got into a gunfight over in Chihuahua and got shot full of lead. I'm letting that be a lesson to me. I keep a very low profile here. You're the first person I've seen from back home. What are you doing here?"

"I did not come looking for you," I told him. "I'm just traveling through, exploring the country, making photographs."

"I saw your name on the wagon outside. I couldn't believe it was really you. That's why I had to come inside and satisfy my curiosity." He rose to his feet to take his leave, "Well, anyway, it was good seeing you again."

"I can't say the same about you. There's a part of me that still wants to kill you. Lucky for you, there's another part that has decided to forgive past transgressions. But there isn't any part of me that wants to be your friend."

"I can understand that. I'm truly sorry for all the harm I've done in my life, especially to you and yours. *Adiós, chica.*"

"*Adiós,*" I repeated. "If you really do intend to go straight, I wish you luck." Silently, I added, *Please, don't make me regret not killing you.*

CHAPTER XXXVII
THE BOOGEYMAN OF THE BORDERLANDS
1888 - 1896

Since making that first great odyssey in my little green wagon, I have spent about half my days at the Bar Double D and the other half on the road, taking photographs and making new friends. I have traveled as far west as Los Angeles and San Francisco, as far north as Denver, and as far east as Hot Springs, Arkansas. I frequently tour northern Chihuahua and Sonora, but I have never again returned to Durango or Sinaloa. I have had it in mind for a while now to make a journey up to New York City and from there down to Washington City, but somehow, I never seem to get around to making that particular trip.

On the evening of September 22, 1888, Charley Cunningham and Charlie Smith quarreled at the French Wine House in Tombstone. What began as an angry disagreement soon became a physical altercation, resulting in the pair's being ejected from the establishment. Out in the street, Cunningham grabbed a pistol from an armed bystander, a Mr Lazard, and shot Smith in the upper thigh, partially crippling him.

Charlie Smith eventually recovered from the gunshot wound and moved away from Tombstone, which was now somewhat in decline, for the mines were having to deal with frequent flooding and occasional fires, even as the price of silver was dropping. In any event, Charlie Smith relocated to the little mining community of Ramsey Canyon in the Huachuca Mountains, where, entering politics for the first time, he was elected councilman. A year or so later, he would marry Margaret Winders, widow of Smith's former mining partner Bob Winders. I lost track of Mr Smith after that.

In 1889, the railroad finally reached Bisbee, which was growing even faster than Tombstone was

declining.   There was still no rail service to Tombstone.

On July 10, 1889, Frank Leslie shot to death
Mollie Williams (known as *Blonde Mollie*), a prosti-
tute who had been living with him at Magnolia
Ranch since his divorce from May Evans.   He was
arrested for murder, tried, convicted, and sentenced
to twenty-five years' incarceration.

When I visited Mr Leslie in jail at the conclusion of his trial,   I didn't really know what to say
to him.   I hated his offense, but I still cared about
him.

"I'm really glad they're not going to hang you,
Mr Leslie," I told him.

"Yeah, me too," he said.   "I can hardly believe
what I have done.   I was blind drunk, jealous, and
filled with uncontrollable rage.   You warned me, I
know, that liquor would be my downfall.   I wish I'd
taken your concern for me more seriously."

On January 9, 1890, Sheriff Slaughter trans-
ported Mr Leslie to Yuma Territorial Prison.   I
have not seen Mr Leslie since, but I did hear in
1896 that Governor Benjamin J Franklin had grant-

ed him a full pardon, and that Mr Leslie had then left Arizona Territory for California.

In 1893, Johnny Behan became chief customs officer in El Paso, Texas.

In 1894, the army decommissioned old Fort Bowie. It is really strange to see all those barracks, officers' homes, stables, and other buildings vacant and beginning to deteriorate. I remember Fort Bowie, at the very mouth of Apache Pass, as a frontier stronghold, busy, vibrant, bustling with activity. Now, it's just a ghost town.

In November of 1894, John Slaughter, having served two terms as sheriff, retired from politics and law enforcement to devote himself exclusively to ranching. Elected to Mr Slaughter's former position was photographer Camillus Sidney Fly, who made Mr Slaughter an honorary deputy. It is a title he holds to this day.

Shortly after the first of the year, I learned that my friend Dahteste, still a prisoner of war, had been transferred to Fort Sill in Oklahoma Territory. I loaded up my little green wagon and struck out to visit her there. I found her in good health. She had contracted and then beaten tuberculosis since last we met. Not many people survive tuberculosis.

Gouyen was also at Fort Sill, but the woman Lozen, whom I had met at Guadalupe Canyon, had died in 1889 at Mount Vernon Barracks in Alabama.

I remained at Fort Sill for two full weeks. I made countless photographs, including pictures of Gouyen, Dahteste, Geronimo, and several other Apaches. I also photographed Indians of other nations. Comanches, in particular, were to be found in great numbers living in close proximity to the fort. I even made portraits of some of the soldiers, officers, and wives.

Meanwhile, the mountains of the Sierra Madre Occidental still shelter scattered pockets of renegade Apaches, who raid isolated farms and ranches in Chihuahua, Sonora, Texas, New Mexico Territory, and Arizona Territory, stealing livestock and household goods. The Apache Kid usually gets the blame for these crimes, even though there has never been a shred of evidence to implicate him. He is a ghost, a legend, the Boogeyman of the Borderlands. More than once, men have claimed to have slain him, but then another raid will occur, and it will, of course, be attributed to the Apache Kid.

On December 3, 1895, an Apache raid on the Merrill farmstead just outside Salmonville resulted in two fatalities. Horatio Merrill and his daughter Elizabeth were both killed. Posses were organized to pursue the marauders. Rewards were offered, but all to no avail.

Then on March 28, 1896, another deadly attack occurred, this one on an isolated cabin at the foot of the Chiricahua Mountains. Slain was Alfred Hands. Blamed, of course, was the Apache Kid.

I happened to be visiting the Slaughters at San Bernardino Ranch when we heard the news.

"I don't believe the Apache Kid is the one carrying out these raids," I said.

When I told my hosts what Eugene Middleton had told me eight years before, they agreed with me that these bloody raids seemed totally out of character with all we knew about the Apache Kid.

Using the San Bernardino Ranch as my base of operations, I began making extended scouting expeditions into the mountains of northern Mexico. If I could locate the renegades' encampment without being discovered, I could return later leading Mr Slaughter and a large posse.

I managed for a while to track a party of eight or nine Apaches, including men, women, and children. Actually, the size of the group changed frequently, as various members left and returned. This little group, probably consisting of two or three families, stayed constantly on the move. They did not seem to have a permanent camp.

Only once did I get close enough to actually see them. Imagine my surprise to recognize amongst their number a warrior by the name of *Massai,* who had surrendered with Geronimo. I had believed him to be a prisoner of war. By the next morning, the entire group had vanished as completely as if they had never existed. There were no further tracks to be found. I returned to San Bernardino Ranch to report what I had learned.

Mr Slaughter was not surprised to hear that Massai was back in our vicinity. "I guess you missed the news that he alone escaped from the train before it ever arrived in Florida. He hasn't been seen since. But this is where he would come. Good work, Gaby."

Meanwhile, the army launched an aggressive campaign to capture or kill whomever was responsible for the murders of the Merrills and Mr Hands. In early May, a patrol led by Second Lieutenant Nathan King Averill of the Seventh Cavalry arrived at San Bernardino Ranch to refill canteens and to camp for the night.

Mr Slaughter asked me to tell the lieutenant what I had observed.

"Massai!" the young officer exclaimed "I'd like to get my hands on that wily bastard. Where did you see them last? And in which direction were they headed?"

"They were in the Guadalupe Mountains about fifty miles south of the international border. They seemed to be meandering aimlessly. If they had any destination in mind, they were in no hurry to arrive. Come to think of it, though, where I lost them was about twenty miles north of where I first picked them up. So very possibly, they are headed, in a roundabout way, for the Animas Valley."

"If you would care to join us, sir," said Lieutenant Averill to Mr Slaughter. "we'll be pulling out at first light."

On the ride to New Mexico, Mr Slaughter rode beside Lieutenant Averill. I rode ahead with the patrol's two Apache scouts. Mr Slaughter's ranch foreman Jesse Fisher and two *pistoleros* in Mr Slaughter's employ followed behind the soldiers. This was only one of dozens of patrols that were currently scouring the Borderlands in search of renegade Apaches.

On May 8, in the Peloncillo Mountains of New Mexico Territory, only a few miles from Lang's Ranch, we came upon the campsite of a small group of Apaches. Apparently, they had seen us coming, for they were already in flight. When they reached the relative safety of a clump of trees, they paused long enough to fire at us. We had not yet fired at them.

But when someone shoots at me, I shoot back. I hit a female warrior, who, dropping her rifle and clutching her side, staggered away out of our sight. We never caught up with her or the others. One Apache man was slightly wounded by the soldiers, and another was shot dead by Mr Slaughter in the initial exchange of gunfire. The man's body fell into a deep chasm and could not be recovered.

The terrain here was frightfully steep with many hiding places, which fact put us at great disadvantage in pursuing the fleeing Apaches. We were forced, for our own safety, to proceed slowly.

Finally, we gave up the chase and returned to the abandoned camp, where we discovered a crying toddler, a girl of about twelve months, naked from the waist down. Her little shirt was made from an election poster printed on muslin.

Mr Slaughter swore that the man he had killed was the Apache Kid. I cannot say whether Mr Slaughter actually believed this to be the case, but the lieutenant seemed to accept the statement as gospel. From the look on the faces of the Apache scouts, I felt sure that they knew the claim to be false, but they kept their mouths shut, and so too did I.

I was given the immediate care of the baby. Leaving the patrol, I delivered my charge to San Bernardino Ranch, there to place her in the arms of Viola Slaughter, who had no children of her own. She was the stepmother to Mr Slaughter's older children, and she and Mr Slaughter had adopted other children as well. They would likewise adopt this little girl and name her *Apache May*. Apache May would be called *Patchy* for short. Patchy, adored by all, would soon become the sweetheart of the entire county.

On May 13, Lieutenant Averill's patrol joined forces with another patrol that was already tracking an Apache party believed to be made up of two men, three women, and one small child. Two days later, the posse caught up with that party at Guadalupe Canyon. The two Apache men were immediately recognized as Massai and Adelnietze.

These two were almost certainly responsible for the murders of Mr Hands and the Merrills, for both were notorious for their ruthless cruelty. Adelnietze had once been with Geronimo's band, but had refused to surrender with the rest.

The only captive taken in this engagement was a five-year-old girl, who was sent to the reservation, presumably to be cared for by relatives there. Adelnietze was wounded (mortally so, it was believed), but not apprehended. Massai and the three women escaped, for again the renegades enjoyed the advantage of position.

CHAPTER XXXVIII
BLACK JACK CHRISTIAN & THE HIGH FIVES
1896 - 1897

The High Fives Gang was led by Black Jack Christian and his brother Bob. The three other gang members were Cole Estes, George Musgrave, and Bob Hayes. All five had been stockmen before becoming outlaws, and all five used various aliases from time to time. The names above are how those five men are best known to me, but may not be their real names.

In 1896, the High Fives Gang rustled cattle, held up banks, stores, and stagecoaches, and robbed trains in the Territories of New Mexico and Arizona. They rarely took breaks between jobs; they were extremely active. Were they in any other line of work, I might describe them as "ambitious" and "industrious." The law was never very far behind them.

On August 1, the gang attempted to rob the International Bank of Nogales in Pima County, Arizona Territory. Nogales, by the way, is no longer in Pima County, but in the recently established Santa Cruz County. In any event, the well-planned robbery was foiled. George Musgrave was wounded in the leg, and two of the gang's horses were shot, one badly enough that it could not be ridden.

Fleeing without the loot they had come for, the gang split up at Beck Canyon. Black Jack Christian and George Musgrave, riding double, headed for a nearby ranch belonging to a friend and confederate, Ed Roberts. The other three outlaws crossed the border into Sonora.

Back in Nogales a posse was organized and led by Customs Agent Samuel F Webb. So eager were the possemen in their pursuit that they did not notice that the horse carrying Musgrave and Black Jack had veered away and was no longer traveling with the others. Had that posse enjoyed the benefit of an expert tracker, two of the robbers could have been apprehended that very day. Instead, the posse followed the other three some fifteen miles into Mexico before losing the trail completely.

Meanwhile, Pima County Sheriff Robert N Leatherwood and two of his deputies, Doyle and Broderick, traveled to Bisbee to meet up with Deputy US Marshal Al Ezekiels and Cochise County Deputies Billy Stiles and Jeff Milton.

Jeff Milton, appreciating the need for a good tracker, invited me along as well. Leaving Bisbee for Nogales, we were joined by Samuel F Webb and those of his posse that had not become too discouraged to continue the hunt. They included another customs agent by the name of *Miller* and two civilian volunteers: Felix Mayhew and a man called *Randolph*. I don't know whether *Randolph* was his first name or last.

In spite of the fact that the earlier posse had partially obliterated the outlaws' tracks, I was able to point out where George Musgarve and Black Jack Christian had separated from the others.

Agent Webb shook his head in consternation. "Damn! I don't see how we missed that."

Here our posse split up, Sheriff Leatherwood, his two deputies and I to follow Black Jack Christian and George Musgrave, the rest led by Marshal Ezekiel to pursue Cole Estes, Bob Christian, and Bob Hayes into Mexico, where they would be joined by forces of the Gendarmería Fiscal (Mexico's customs service) under the command of General Juan Fenochio. This enormous posse would twice catch sight of the three bandits, but never get close enough to engage them.

I was easily able to track the two outlaws riding double to the Roberts Ranch. The sheriff and his deputies searched the main house and all the out buildings whilst I rode ever-widening circles around the ranch yard trying to determine in which direction the two outlaws had traveled from here. But this was a busy place. I could identify tracks of at least a dozen pairs of riders that had left the ranch yard in the past twenty-four hours.

"I don't have a clue," I was forced to admit.

"Let's ride south to the border and there turn eastward," the sheriff said. "I figure they'll eventually head back to New Mexico Territory, where they are more at home."

We soon encountered Cochise County Sheriff CS Fly and a posse from Tombstone. Not long after that we were re-joined by Deputy Milton. I was relieved, for Milton was the only one of these men that really wanted me along.

Eventually, we picked up the trail of Cole Estes, Bob Hayes, and Bob Christian. Tracking them was easy now. They were heading into Guadalupe Canyon, also called *Skeleton Canyon*. From there, they might make their way into New Mexico Territory or Mexico.

"This is as far as we can go," I told Sheriff Fly "That canyon is a death trap. It would take a whole company of cavalry to rout those three men out of there, and casualties would be enormous."

Deputy Milton was no longer with us. He and some others had ridden off in search of fresh mounts. He would have advised the sheriff to heed my advice.

"If you're not up to this, Miss Falcón," said the sheriff, "you are more than welcome to return to Tombstone now. I don't remember inviting you along anyway."

"Jeff Milton asked for my help," I told him. "I wish that he were here now. He'd tell you that I know what I'm talking about."

Argument was pointless. In the end, I left the posse and turned back just as they rode into that canyon that had seen so many deadly ambushes before.

Remarkably, the posse suffered but one casualty. Frank Robson, in the lead, was shot twice in the head. The rest of the possemen immediately sought cover and remained pinned down until after dark. During the night, the three outlaws managed to slip away unseen.

Black Jack Christian later sent the widow of Inspector Robson money with his apology for his men's having killed her husband. He reminded her that he himself had not been present.

The High Fives were just about the slipperiest bunch of outlaws I've ever known about. But luck was about to run out for some of them.

On October 2, 1896, the gang attempted to rob a train at Rio Puerco, New Mexico Territory. The robbery was foiled and Cole Estes was killed by Deputy US Marshal Will Loomis, who happened to be a passenger on that train.

On November 18, Bob Hayes was killed by lawman Fred Higgins at the Diamond A Ranch in the San Simon Valley of Southwest New Mexico Territory.

On April 27, 1897, Black Jack Christian himself was slain in a firefight with lawmen at a cave hideout near Clifton, Arizona Territory.

Bob Christian and George Musgrave, as far as I know, are still at large.

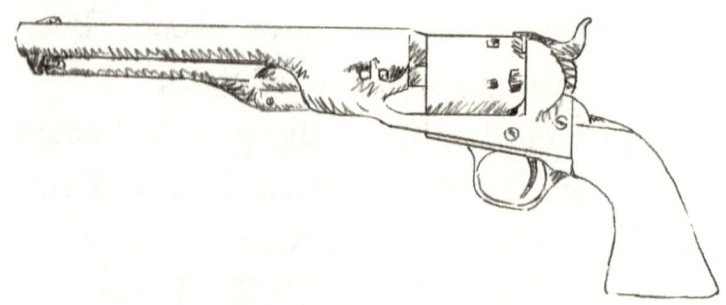

CHAPTER IXL
PEARL HART & JOE BOOT
1898 - 1899

A little less than two years ago, in the autumn of 1898, I became one of the first individuals in the territory to buy a motor carriage. My various investments having made me quite comfortably well off, I quibbled not at paying a thousand dollars for an elegant new Winton, one of the first twenty-two ever produced.

And what a beauty it is! With an eight-horsepower hydrocarbon engine, it easily achieves speeds in excess of twenty miles per hour. It seats four comfortably, the rear pair of seats facing backward.

Mind you, I rarely operate the Winton myself. I bought it for my father, who, with his injured hip, still experiences a significant level of pain when riding a horse. Firing up the Winton is a lot easier for him than hitching a team to a wagon.

"I love this horseless carriage, Gaby," Papa confided after his first solo trip in it to Tombstone. "I can't thank you enough, but I aim to kill the next son-of-a-bitch that addresses me as *Mr Rockefeller*."

The Bar Double D had now become quite profitable since we changed our business plan from capturing mustangs to breeding horses. Our monthly bill for hay and oats amounts to a small fortune, but the investment pays off in the end. Our beautiful animals, all descended from Nube de Truenos, are much in demand.

Modesta's goat-ranching operation has proven quite successful as well. As her herd has grown, so too have the financial rewards.

As for my photography, that, I must admit, is a different story. I barely break even. The problem is that my hobby of landscape photography consumes all the profits generated by my portrait business. Even so, I never want for anything, and I have no serious money problems. So I guess it doesn't really matter all that much.

In the spring of 1899, I was on top of the world. The last thing I ever expected was to be arrested for stagecoach robbery.

As susceptible to robbery and collapse as banks are, it never makes sense to allow one's wealth to accumulate in a single bank. Every year or so, as our ranch became more and more profitable, we established new accounts in various banks throughout the territory.

It was for the purpose of opening a new bank account that I traveled north on June 2, to the town of Florence in Pinal County. Tying my horse at a hitching rail, I entered the bank and asked to see an officer.

"Have a seat, miss," I was told. "Someone will be right with you."

Five minutes later, Sheriff Truman—I never heard his given name—and three deputies entered the lobby with guns drawn. At first, I thought it was a holdup. I leapt to my feet and drew my own revolver.

"Hold it right there, miss!" the sheriff shouted. "Don't make me shoot you."

With four cocked revolvers pointed at me, I gently lowered the hammer of my own gun and raised my hands. The sheriff stepped forward to take the Navy Colt dangling from my finger. I was then marched to jail, dozens of onlookers crowding around to observe my parade of shame. Before being put into a cell, I was pat-searched and relieved of my gunbelt and my concealed Derringer.

"My apologies for taking such liberties with your person," the sheriff said, blushing a deep scarlet, "but it had to be done."

"I reckon I'll live over it," I replied. "May I ask why you have arrested me?"

It seemed that the stagecoach operating between Florence and Globe City had recently been held up by two bandits, one of whom closely matched my description.

"Matched my description how?" I asked.

The sheriff read aloud from a witness statement, "'...a slender young woman wearing men's clothing and wielding a .38 like she knowed how to use it and wouldn't hesitate to do so.'"

"A woman held up the stagecoach?" I asked, incredulous. "And you think it was I?"

"Are you saying that it wasn't you?" the sheriff asked.

"Absolutely! When exactly did this holdup occur? Maybe I can furnish you with an alibi."

"Mid-afternoon two days ago."

"May 30, right?"

"That's right."

I wracked my brain, trying to recall where I had been that afternoon. Suddenly, it occurred to me that I had a receipt in my pocket that would prove that I had been in Bisbee that day. Bisbee is about a hundred seventy-five miles from Florence. I handed that receipt to the sheriff.

"This is signed by Jeff Milton," Sheriff Truman observed. "I know him. I'll have to wire him for a confirmation."

"You might ask him for a character reference too. My name is *Gabriela Falcón*, but most folks in Tombstone know me as *Little Durango*. I've been the tracker for two different posses that Jeff Milton was a part of."

"I'll do that, but as late as it already is, you're probably going to have to spend the night in jail. I'll do everything I can to make you comfortable and to give you some privacy. I truly do hope that Milton comes through for you."

By noon the next day, I was again a free woman. Furthermore, I had been engaged by the sheriff to track the actual bandits.

"We followed them for miles and miles," one of the deputies confided to me as we mounted up. "They seemed to be wandering around aimlessly, but little by little their trail got harder to pick out, and eventually we lost it altogether."

"If we don't get a big rain first, I'll find them for you," I promised.

Our posse consisted of Sheriff Truman, two deputies, and me. It took us two and a half days to overtake our quarry. It was well after dark on the evening of June 5, when we came upon their campsite. The two outlaws were fast asleep.

Prodded awake with a pistol, the man, Joe Boot, surrendered peacefully. The woman, Pearl Hart, fought like a wildcat and might have got away had I not knocked her unconscious with the barrel of my pistol. When she came to her senses, she was in irons.

Neither the sheriff nor the deputies had been able to bring themselves to strike her. I suffered from no such compunction.

I later read that Pearl Hart had escaped. Then a short while later, I read that she had been re-captured. At trial, the two defendants were acquitted, for Pearl Hart had become something of a celebrity and a public sweetheart. One admirer made her a present of a bobcat kitten for a pet, which she kept in her cell with her. Joe Boot managed to skate by on Pearl Hart's popularity.

Shortly after being released, the two were re-arrested on federal charges of interfering with the mail. At their second trial, Joe Boot was sentenced to thirty years; Pearl Hart, to five years. I doubt she'll have to do it all.

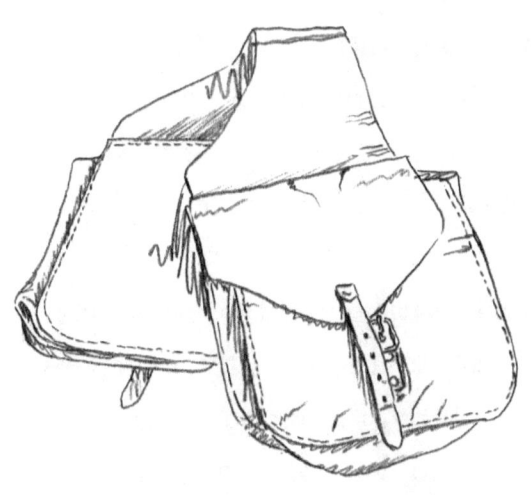

CHAPTER XL

FIN DE SIÈCLE

1900

Having, earlier this year, celebrated my thirty-first birthday and being still unwed, I suppose I must acknowledge that I am now officially an old maid. It is not that no man has ever proposed to me. My suitors have been many and include cattlemen, officers of the law, soldiers, army scouts, and miners. All were lacking either the power of personality to capture my interest or else the character and integrity that would have allowed me to deem them worthy.

Mind you, there have been men of my acquaintance whose courtship I should have welcomed were those men not already married or engaged to someone else. Life—or Fate perhaps—can be so perverse.

I don't usually mind being single, but sometimes—if I am to be perfectly honest—I do get to feeling a bit lonely. Even so, it is better by far to be alone than to be with the wrong person. At least, that is how it seems to me.

Now, before I bring this narrative to a close, I must relate a couple of recent developments, about which, I believe, Dear Reader, you will wish to be informed.

Deputy Sheriff Burt Alford was arrested last spring in connection with a train robbery, only to be broken out of jail a short time later by one of his accomplices. Burt, you will recall, was the boy with whom I skipped school on the day of the Earps' big gunfight with the cowboys back in '81. For more than a year now, Burt has apparently been the mastermind behind a gang of train robbers.

In February of this year, in Fairbank, formerly known as *Junction City*, Jeff Milton, working as an express messenger for Southern Pacific Railroad, foiled an attempted train robbery by Burt's gang, wounding two of the holdup men and being wounded himself.

Shortly thereafter, four of the outlaws were apprehended by Sheriff Scott White. One of the captured outlaws, Three-Fingered Jack Dunlop, as he lay dying in hospital, revealed that Burt Alford was the gang's secret leader. Dunlop further implicated Deputy Sheriff Billy Stiles, who then made a full confession and confirmed Dunlop's accusation against Burt Alford. Cattleman William Downing (a former member of the Sam Bass Gang) has also been arrested for furnishing the gang with dynamite. Burt himself is still at large, but I doubt that he will remain so for long.

In July of this year, Warren Earp was shot to death. After returning to Arizona a few years ago, he showed himself to be a mean-spirited bully, completely unlike any of his older brothers. In recent years, he has been working as a range detective for Mr Hooker. That was the same job that Papa used to do for Mr Hooker when I was a small child. In Willcox the other day, Warren challenged Mr

Hooker's range boss Tommy Boyett to a gunfight, and Boyett killed him.

Willcox, by the way, is the same little town in the Sulphur Springs Valley that used to be called *Maley*. It was renamed in 1889 in honor of a visiting dignitary, General Orlando Willcox.

I plan next spring to strike out in my little green wagon for California, there to take ship (with the wagon) for Alaska, where any number of old friends now abide, amongst them Wyatt Earp, Josephine Marcus (now known as *Mrs Wyatt Earp*), former Tombstone mayor John Clum, and Miss Nellie. What a grand reunion we shall have! And oh, the photographs I mean to make! I can barely endure to wait until next spring to get underway.

My little sister Val (now seventeen years old) has expressed a desire to go with me. I should adore to have her company on this marvelous adventure, but Papa and Marietta have yet to give their permission. Val, being much more biddable than I ever was, will not go without their consent. I am, therefore, keeping my fingers crossed that Papa and Marietta will decide to trust me to keep Val safe and out of trouble.

AFTERWORD
Regarding the Historical Accuracy
of this Narrative

I wrote this novel during the height of the pandemic whilst I was under strict lockdown in England. My research was, therefore, limited to those books and documents already in my possession and to internet sites, which cannot always be depended upon. Usually, I try to verify every fact uncovered by tracking down primary sources; on this occasion, that was impossible. Even so, I believe that I have presented known historical facts with a high degree of accuracy. At least, that was my intention.

Mind you, I did exercise my creative imagination in dealing with certain historical mysteries. For instance, on the night before the Gunfight at the OK Corral, it is known that Virgil Earp played cards with Sheriff Behan, Ike Clanton, Tom McLaury, and one other man, whose identity is now unknown. I simply identified him as Durango Falcón.

In another instance, I created a fiction to explain away two separate mysteries that occurred around the same time: namely, the disappearance of Hank Swilling and the unidentified body found in the ruins of the burned-out Cosmopolitan Hotel.

As for the killing of Johnny Ringo, no one really knows for sure how that came about. My version—and this cannot be said of most other fictional accounts—accommodates all the known facts of the case.

Another historical mystery is what happened with Pony Diehl after his release from prison. I merely speculated that he might very well have drifted down to Mexico and there kept a low profile, having become somewhat wiser during his incarceration. That is as likely a scenario as any other.

The only liberty I took with facts that might possibly be established by digging through old census records is with what became of Marietta Duarte (wife of Pete Spence) and her mother, whose actual name, by the way, I was unable to ascertain. After giving evidence against Pete Spence and his cronies, Marietta and her mother seem to have disappeared from history. I gave the mother a name and a back story. Then, I simply allowed those two women to continue interacting with my fictional heroine and her father.

One other thing I must mention: It is my firm belief that Frank Patterson the outlaw cowboy and Frank Patterson the Tombstone businessman and property owner are two separate individuals. I must acknowledge, however, that I could be wrong about that. Were I actually in Arizona going through old records, I might well establish the truth of the matter, but at the moment, I am still trapped overseas.

M W Ashe